Getting in

The first day of school is always ~~~~~~~~~~~~~~ t as she checked her schedule to see where her next class was. It was maths, and the room was close by. Becka took a seat in the back of the room, where she had a good view of her classmates as they poured in.

She was starting to figure out exactly which people fitted into which group. There were girls who dressed like Cat, and wore make-up; Cat wouldn't have any problem finding friends. She never had a problem. And there were lots of kids, both boys and girls, who looked like jocks; Josie would be sure to hang out with them.

But that was okay, Becka decided. They didn't all have to like the same people. Becka would just figure out a way to make friends of her own. How hard could that be, anyway? If people didn't like her the way she was . . . well, she'd just be somebody else.

Will the Real Becka Morgan Please Stand Up?

Marilyn Kaye

Lions

Lions, an imprint of HarperCollins *Children's Books*

For Roberta, Jeff,
Laura and Julie Malickson

First published in the U.S. in 1991
by HarperCollins Books.
First published in the U.K. in Lions in 1992

Lions is an imprint of
HarperCollins Children's Books,
part of HarperCollins Publishers Ltd,
77–85 Fulham Palace Road, Hammersmith, London W6 8JB

Printed and bound in Great Britain by
HarperCollins Manufacturing Ltd, Glasgow

One

Becka looked down at her plate, where three slices of golden brown French toast lay in a pool of sweet Vermont maple syrup. It was her all-time favourite breakfast. But she didn't think she'd be able to eat a bite.

She looked across the table at Cat and Josie. Josie was attacking her meal with gusto, and Cat seemed to be enjoying hers, too. How could they possibly eat on a day like this?

Her own lack of interest in her food didn't go unnoticed. "Becka, aren't you hungry?" Annie asked.

"Not really," Becka admitted. "I guess I'm just too excited to eat."

Cat daintily touched a napkin to her lips. "Honestly, Becka. It's just the first day of school. You act like you've never gone to school before."

"Not *this* school," Becka replied. "Doesn't starting a new school make you guys feel anything?"

"Yeah," Josie said. "Hungry. And if the lunches at Green Falls Junior High are like the ones back at our old school, you'd better fill up now."

"I wish I could," Becka said mournfully. She cut off a small piece and chewed it slowly. "This is great, Josie."

"Better than great," Ben said. "It's incredible." He helped himself to seconds. "I've never had French toast this good, Josie. No offence," he added hastily to his wife.

"None taken," Annie responded with a laugh. "I'm the first to admit Josie has us all beat when it comes to cooking. But you didn't need to fix breakfast on the first day of school, honey."

Josie grinned. "No problem. I don't get all worked up about school. Not like Becka."

"Becka *loves* school," Cat said, her tone making it perfectly clear what she thought of that.

"You probably would, too, if you made all As," Josie pointed out.

"All As," Cat repeated thoughtfully. "That's kind of like showing off, isn't it?"

"I wouldn't mind seeing a little showing off like that," Ben noted.

Becka beamed. For once, she didn't mind Cat's teasing. She *did* make all As, and she was proud of it. She wasn't a genius, but she never minded studying, or writing essays, or even taking tests. Of course, she liked some subjects more than others. English homework was definitely preferable to maths.

"How's my hair?" Cat asked.

"Very nice," Annie said. "I like the way the hairdresser trimmed it around your face. Your eyes stand out." She looked around the table. "You all look lovely."

Becka adjusted the big collar of her sailor-style blouse. She and Annie had spent a great day at Encore, an antique clothing place where Becka had found just the kind of unusual clothes that she liked. She thought the navy blue blouse and skirt made her look taller and thinner. Fingering a lock of her blonde hair, she hoped it wouldn't frizz in the humidity.

Josie wriggled in her chair. "I should have washed these jeans a few more times to break them in."

Cat spoke in a mildly reproving tone. "I can't believe you're wearing jeans today. I mean, they're okay for later on, but for the first day of school? . . ."

"I thought the first day of school wasn't all that important to you," Ben said teasingly.

Cat gave him one of her beguiling smiles. "I still want to look my best."

And she did, Becka had to admit. Cat always looked pretty, but today she'd outdone herself. Her glossy black hair shone like ebony, and Becka knew from magazine covers that Cat's long top and short skirt were the height of fashion. And the emerald colour made her large eyes look even greener than they normally did.

Josie was her usual self, though the new jeans and clean, ironed shirt made her look a little neater. And the new short haircut had tamed her wild red hair. Actually, the look suited her boyish appearance. No one would guess she was a wizard in the kitchen, though they might suspect her other passion- sports.

We certainly don't look like sisters, Becka thought. And much as she tried, it was hard to *feel* like sisters. But maybe that was understandable. After all, only two months ago, they'd been unrelated orphans. Their only connection was that they'd shared a room at the Willoughby Hall Home for Children practically all their lives.

Then, into their lives had come Annie and Ben Morgan, looking to adopt an older girl. After meeting Becka, Cat, and Josie, they decided to adopt *three*. And suddenly they were sisters. They still shared a room, but now they had more in common – parents. And the identical little ruby rings Annie and Ben had given them to symbolise their birth as a family.

Still, they were all so different. Cat was beautiful and Josie was a great athlete. But it was in school that Becka would shine. And school was starting today.

"Are you going to miss us?" Cat asked Annie and Ben.

"Are you kidding?" Ben wiggled his eyebrows up and down. "Don't you know school was invented to keep parents from losing their minds?"

"Stop that," Annie scolded him. "The girls might think you mean it."

Becka gave Ben a reassuring shake of her head. The girls hadn't been with the Morgans for long, but they were already used to Ben's teasing. That was one of the easy things to get used to. Some things had been a lot harder. Becka remembered how Cat had behaved those first few weeks at the Morgans'. She had been so thrilled by the lack of rules and regulations, she'd taken advantage of the situation: skipping out when she was supposed to be working at the family store, Morgan's Country Foods, being late for meals, showing up whenever she felt like it. It had taken a family heart-to-heart talk for Cat to realise that daughters *did* have responsibilities.

Josie had had a hard time adjusting, too, Becka recalled. She was sure she'd be sent back to the orphanage, since that was what had happened three other times when she was almost adopted. She was so positive she'd be sent back that she took matters into her own hands and ran away, back to Willoughby Hall. But she came back, and finally accepted the fact that this was her real, permanent home.

As for herself . . . the memory made Becka's face start to burn. She had been intent on creating the perfect family, like the kind she read about in books. When she found out she was allergic to Aurora, the family kitten, she felt less than perfect. Knowing how much Annie loved Aurora, Becka had tried to hide her rash, her wheezes, and her red eyes. It had been a thrilling relief when she discovered that her health was a lot more important to her parents than a pet.

"Earth to Becka, come in, Becka," Josie said.

Becka blinked. "Oh, sorry. I was daydreaming."

"How unusual," Cat murmured, with just the slightest touch of sarcasm.

But Annie smiled. "What were you thinking about?"

"Us. Being a family."

Annie's wistful eyes swept over the three girls. "*I'll* miss you. Every book I've read on parenting says mothers and fathers feel an aching sense of loss when their children go off to school for the first time. And they were right."

Ben scratched his forehead. "I think those books were referring to toddlers starting nursery school. Not thirteen-year-olds going into eighth grade."

"It's the same for us," Annie insisted. "After all, we've only had our daughters for two months. I can't help it. I feel something."

"Okay, okay," Ben said. "I'll confess. I'm going to miss you guys, too."

"What are you going to do all day without us?" Becka asked.

"I'm going to work in the store," Annie said. "Who knows? Maybe we'll actually get a few customers."

"And I'm going to start stripping the floors upstairs," Ben told them. "With any luck, we'll have another livable room in a few weeks."

Three heads jerked up at that announcement. "Will that mean another bedroom for us?" Cat asked.

Annie nodded. "You girls have been great about sharing. But I firmly believe a teenage girl needs a room of her own. And you'll each have one eventually."

"Unfortunately, we can only afford to renovate one room at a time," Ben said.

Josie, in her usual blunt way, asked the question on all their minds. "Who's going to get this one?"

Annie and Ben exchanged looks, then Annie spoke for both of them. "We think you girls should decide that among yourselves."

Cat smiled. Josie nodded. Becka just sighed and went back to poking at her food. There was no point in even dreaming about the possibility of her own private bedroom. Between Cat and Josie . . . well, when it came to standing up for herself, she wasn't exactly in their league.

She managed to get down a few more bites of French toast before Ben announced it was time to leave. "Annie or I will drive you to school in the mornings," he said. "But we thought you wouldn't mind walking home."

"Most days you'll probably have after-school plans anyway," Annie added. "School activities, seeing your friends . . ."

"Or going to the library," Becka added. She enjoyed the pleased expressions on her parents' faces and ignored the look Cat and Josie gave each other. In her mind, she saw herself bringing report cards home to rapturous cries of delight.

Annie wasn't kidding when she said how much she'd miss them. Her eyes were just a little wet as she kissed the girls goodbye, and the three of them left with Ben. They went down the front steps, carefully avoiding the one with the ominous creak.

"This house needs so much work," Ben muttered as they walked to the car. Becka looked back at the old, grey, weather-beaten farmhouse. It was hard for her to really see the shabbiness. So what if it was a little rundown? It was home.

It was a short drive to the low, modern building that was Green Falls Junior High. "Have a good day," Ben called as the girls scrambled out of the battered blue station wagon.

Josie saluted him, stuck her hands in her pockets, and strode towards the door. Cat blew him a kiss, then waved to a pretty black girl who was standing by the entrance. The girl waved back and waited for Cat to join her.

Becka hesitated by the car. "Is something wrong?" Ben asked.

Becka managed a thin smile. It was always hard for her to walk into a strange place alone.

But this is a school, she reminded herself. How strange could a school be?

"I'm fine," she assured Ben. "See you later!"

She'd been in the building once before, for registration. But today, the crowds and the noise made it seem like a whole different place, a labyrinth of corridors. Becka consulted her schedule. Homeroom was in room C-128. She followed the signs that led to C hall.

Peering through the window of the door to her homeroom, she saw boys and girls gathered in tight little groups. A girl brushed past her, mumbling, "Excuse me," as she opened the door and went in. Becka could see her being greeted by one of the groups and welcomed into their circle.

Becka took a deep breath and slipped inside. She slid into a seat near the door, trying to be inconspicuous. She needn't have worried. Nobody noticed her arrival.

She looked around. The room was identical to every other classroom she'd been in. There was the teacher's desk up front, a clean blackboard, and rows of chairs with attached desks, most of them still empty while students took advantage of the few minutes left before the bell rang.

Becka did notice one other occupied seat, towards the back. A small, thin girl with an uneven fringe touching the rims of large glasses sat there. She was carefully labelling the dividers in her three-ring notebook. *She must be new, too*, Becka thought. She caught the girl's eye

13

and smiled. The girl smiled back briefly and returned to her labelling.

The bell rang. The students scrambled into their seats as a tall, dark-haired man came in and went to the teacher's desk, where he placed a stack of papers. Becka sat up straight and gave him her undivided attention, which wasn't difficult. He was so handsome. Green Falls Junior High was looking better and better. The teacher smiled. Becka smiled back.

"Good morning," he said.

"Good morning," Becka replied. The sound of her voice echoed in the room, and it was followed by a snicker from somewhere behind her. A blush crept up her neck as she realised she was the only one who'd responded to the teacher's greeting.

"I'm Mr Davison," the man began, but before he could go on, there was a crackling sound from the intercom above his head. It was followed by a voice Becka recognised from registration.

"Good morning, boys and girls. This is your principal, Dr Potter. Welcome back to a new term at Green Falls Junior High. I'm sure you're all looking forward to an enjoyable and productive school year."

He went on to give the same kind of first-day-of-school speech Becka had heard before, but she paid attention anyway. Towards the end, he said, "Throughout the week, you'll be hearing about many of our extracurricular activities. After school today, there will be meetings of the chess club, the drama club, and the newspaper staff. Later this week, there will be auditions for the chorus. I encourage you to take advantage of these opportunities to explore your interests and get involved with your school."

Extracurricular activities. Back at her old school, Becka hadn't been involved with any after-school events. It was too much of a hassle, getting permission from Mrs Scanlon at Willoughby Hall, arranging for a counsellor to pick her up. But all that was different now. She could actually participate in school activities.

Thinking about this, she was dimly aware that the principal had finished his announcements, and Mr Davison was taking roll. What would she be interested in? The drama club? The chorus? There were so many options!

"Morgan? Morgan? Becka Morgan?"

"Oh! Here." Becka had no idea how many times he'd called her name. Behind her, she heard the snickers again, and the blush that hadn't quite gone away deepened. She had to cut out this daydreaming. It was hard enough recognising a name she'd only had for two months.

When the roll call was finished, Mr Davison handed out cards listing their locker numbers and combinations. Then he picked up the stack of papers on his desk. "As usual, there are lots of forms to be filled out. Let's see, there are state forms, county forms, medical forms . . . I hope you guys like writing your name."

Becka did. She still got a thrill writing down *Becka Morgan* instead of *Becka Blue*. This time, for the first time ever, she wouldn't have to leave the spaces for her parents' names blank. Happily, with firm strokes, she pencilled in the names of Annie and Ben Morgan.

Filling out forms took up the whole period. When the bell rang, Becka checked her schedule for the location of her next class, maths. It turned out to be close by, and she was the first student in the room. This time she took a seat in the back. From there, she had a good view of her classmates as they poured in.

She recognised a couple of them from her homeroom. As the room filled, once again they formed small tight groups that held together until the teacher walked in.

It was the same in her next class, biology. By this time, Becka was starting to figure out what the members of each group had in common. There were girls who dressed like Cat in one group. They wore make-up, and they all had nice hairstyles. Another group contained both boys and girls, and they all looked very serious. A bunch of boys who wore sweaters with the letter *G* on them formed another group.

Having her two hardest subjects first wasn't exactly Becka's idea of a good time, but she was glad to get them out of the way. Her spirits were high as she headed towards her next class, English.

In the room, she spotted the girl she'd noticed

in homeroom, the one who had sat alone. She slid into the seat next to her.

"Hi, my name's Becka Morgan."

The girl peered at her over her glasses. "I'm Louise Nolan."

"Where are you from?" Becka asked.

Louise looked confused. "What do you mean?"

"Where did you live before you came here?"

"I've always lived here in Green Falls," Louise said.

"Oh, I thought you just moved here, like me."

"Why'd you think that?"

Becka fumbled with her words. "Well, I, uh, saw you in homeroom, and you weren't talking to anyone."

"Oh, I know just about everyone in this school," Louise told her. "But I don't hang out with them. I guess I'm what they call a loner. I'm not into groups."

Becka looked around at the circles that had formed while they were talking. "What kind of groups are they, anyway?"

Louise considered them. "Well, those are the popular girls over there. That bunch wearing jeans are the farm kids. The guys with the letter sweaters are the jocks. The really cute one is Todd Murphy. He's co-captain of the football team *and* captain of the basketball team."

Becka was absorbing all this information when the teacher entered. Everyone took a seat, and Becka pushed all thoughts of the groups from her mind and focused on the woman standing before them.

"I'm Ms Levin, and I'll be your English teacher this term. I'm very excited about our new curriculum, which will combine both reading and creative writing."

Becka thought she'd died and gone to heaven. She listened eagerly as Ms Levin described what they'd be doing. "We're going to start with biography and autobiography. Autobiography is the story of one's own life. Biography is the history of someone's life told by someone else." As she went on, Becka felt shivers run through her. Ms Levin was fantastic. Before long, Becka decided she'd be her absolutely favourite teacher of all time.

"Unfortunately, our textbooks aren't here yet," Ms Levin said. "But you won't need them for your first assignment, which is due on Thursday." She disregarded the muffled groans that went through the room. "Each of you will write a one-page autobiography. And don't try to tell me that your life is too boring to write about. Any life is interesting. It all depends on how you describe it."

Just then, the door opened and the principal's secretary, Ms Sanders, came in. She conferred in a whisper with Ms Levin, who then turned back to the class. "It seems our textbooks have arrived. I'm going to get them now." With a smile, she added, "I'd ask you to be quiet while I'm gone, but I know that's impossible."

She was right. As soon as she left, kids jumped up from their seats and formed their groups.

"I'm going to love this class," Becka told Louise. "Ms Levin seems nice. English is my favourite subject anyway."

"Yeah?" Louise wrinkled her nose. "It's my worst. I'm just not into books. And I hate writing essays."

Becka felt sorry for anyone who didn't like reading. Cat and Josie weren't into books either. That was one of the many things about them she'd never understand. But she tried not to look too dismayed. "What subjects do you like?"

"Any kind of science," Louise said promptly. "I'm going to be a doctor. Not just a regular doctor, though. I want to do medical research and discover cures for diseases."

Becka was impressed and was about to say so when Ms Levin returned. She distributed the textbooks and assigned the reading for tomorrow. Then the bell rang.

"Do you have lunch now?" Becka asked Louise hopefully.

"No, study hall."

"Oh. Too bad." Becka got up. "I guess I'll see you later."

She found the lunchroom without any difficulty. What *was* difficult was getting up the nerve to walk in. From the entrance, she eyed the crowds nervously. Kids were gathering at long tables, greeting each other loudly, and acting like they knew exactly where they were supposed to be.

Becka joined the line to get her lunch tray. When she emerged from the counter area, her eyes scanned the room. She saw Cat, already sitting at a table with a bunch of girls, talking and laughing. She could have sworn their eyes met for a split second, but Cat didn't show any evidence of having seen her.

Becka made her way to an empty table. It didn't really bother her to eat alone. She had done it all the time back at her old school. And she'd brought a book to read while she ate.

Even so, as she took another peek at Cat and her group, she couldn't help feeling a twinge of envy.

Two

"There's a girl looking at you," Marla said.

Cat looked up, then quickly looked away.

"Do you know her?" Marla asked.

"Yeah, that's Becka. She's my – one of the other girls the Morgans adopted." She poked her fork at the food on her plate. "What *is* this stuff?"

Trisha Heller laughed. "That's one of the great mysteries of Green Falls Junior High."

"Hey, you want to invite Becka to sit with us?" Sharon Cohen asked.

Cat's eyes shifted briefly towards Becka again. No, she didn't want Becka to sit here. She couldn't even imagine her with this group. Trisha was so elegant, with her neat, cropped dark hair and her crisp shirtdress, which Cat knew carried a designer label. Sharon was more casual in a jumpsuit, her long, straight brown hair falling over her shoulders, but she had a look that was undeniably right. And always-chic Marla was particularly sophisticated today, her white linen blouse providing a striking contrast to her dark skin and black curls. No, sitting with frumpy Becka was out of the question. But she couldn't think of a way to say that to the girls without sounding really mean.

Luckily for Cat, there was a distraction. A skinny, short-haired boy with wire-rimmed glasses was approaching, and the girls at Cat's table greeted him enthusiastically. "Jason, this is Cat Morgan," Marla said. "She's new here. Cat, Jason's the editor of the *Green Gazette*, the school newspaper."

"Hi," Cat said. "Nice to meet you."

"Same here. Where are you from?"

This was the question Cat always dreaded. It always felt awkward, trying to explain.

Marla spoke up for her. "She's just been adopted, by Annie and Ben Morgan. You know, the couple from New York who own Morgan's Country Foods."

Jason's eyebrows popped up over the rim of his glasses. "Hey, that's really interesting." He whipped out a little pad and pencil from his back pocket. "What was your name again?"

Cat told him and he wrote it down. "I'm thinking of doing a series of articles about new students with interesting backgrounds. Maybe with photos. I'll be in touch." With a wave, he took off.

Marla looked pleased. "Well, *that* should turn you into a celebrity. And I know someone who wouldn't be too thrilled about it." She cocked her head, indicating a table just behind them.

Cat could have guessed who she was talking about before she looked. Heather Beaumont sat there with a group of girls. They were all listening raptly to whatever the pretty, blonde girl was telling them.

Just seeing her made Cat clench her fists. "I still can't believe she tricked me into getting Ms Gold for English." Marla knew the story, but Cat explained to Sharon and Trisha. "When I came here to register, she was in the principal's office. Just trying to be friendly, I asked her if she could recommend any easy teachers. She told me to get Gold for English. How was I supposed to know she was the toughest teacher in the whole school?"

"Have you had that class yet?" Marla asked, her huge brown eyes warm with sympathy.

"First period this morning. She *piled* on the homework. Can you believe it? Homework on the first day of school? I thought there was a law against that."

"That's Ms Gold for you," Trisha said. "Everyone knows about her. That was a rotten thing for Heather to do to you. But typical." She made a face. "Look at her. She acts like she's a queen holding court with her subjects."

"And here comes her king," Sharon noted.

Todd Murphy, with two other boys, was making his way towards the food line. Cat threw a sidelong look at Heather. She had her eyes fixed on Todd.

"But he might not be her king for long," Marla said. "Tell them, Cat."

23

Cat told Trisha and Sharon how she'd manoeuvred a few meetings with Todd, even getting him to take her to Brownies, the junior high hangout in town, after a football practice. "Heather's friend Blair was there, and saw us. So I'm sure Heather knows, too."

Trisha grinned in delight. "Boy, I'd love to see you snatch Todd right out of her claws."

Cat watched as Todd emerged from the counter with his tray. Then she leaned forward. "Watch this." Todd was coming down the aisle, and he was going to have to pass right by Cat before he got to Heather. Cat lowered her eyes, watched his feet, and judged his pace. At precisely the right moment, she rose.

"Oh! I'm sorry."

Todd balanced the tray that was tilting precariously from Cat's gentle collision. "That's okay." He gave her that crooked grin she found so appealing. "How ya doing?"

"Pretty good," Cat said, giving her head a toss so her hair bounced on her shoulders. "How about you?"

"Well, you know, first day of school and all that . . ."

Cat laughed as if he'd just said something witty. "I know what you mean."

"Todd!" Heather appeared by his side. "We're sitting over there."

"Yeah, okay," Todd said, but his eyes were still on Cat. "See ya later."

Cat smiled and nodded, as if his words had

some special significance. She kept the smile in place as Heather shot her a baleful look.

"Not bad," Marla said with approval as Cat returned to her seat.

"Better be careful, though," Trisha cautioned. "Heather always figures out a way to get back at people who stand in her way."

Cat's face was all innocence. "I was just saying hello to Todd."

"It's not what you said," Sharon replied with a grin. "It's the way you said it." They all started laughing.

"Ooh, look at her," Marla whispered. "She's mad. I can tell from her expression."

Casually, Cat dropped her napkin. Bending down to get it, she sneaked a peek at Heather's table. Satisfied that her little encounter with Todd had made an impact, she retrieved the napkin. But as she straightened up, her eyes rested on Becka for a second.

What a depressing sight. Becka looked so pathetic, sitting over there by herself with her nose pressed against a book. And that awful blouse she was wearing . . .

"Cat? What's the matter?"

Cat turned back to Marla. "Nothing," she said. "Everything's perfect."

Sitting on a bench in the dressing room, Josie laced up her tennis shoes. Near her, two girls were talking as they stuffed their clothes into their lockers.

"I hope we don't have to climb ropes this year," the chubby girl with long, straight brown hair said.

"Yeah," the other girl agreed. "Last year, I couldn't get more than three feet up."

"You did better than me. I couldn't move. I just *hung* there."

"Ropes aren't so bad," Josie said. "The trick is to concentrate on keeping your knees locked."

The girls looked at her with interest. "Maybe you can help us. Miss Connors isn't real good about giving individual attention."

"I'll be glad to," Josie said. She noticed a tennis racket in one girl's locker. "Are you on the tennis team?"

The girl nodded as she pulled her light brown hair back into a ponytail. "You play?"

"No, I like team sports. Basketball, softball, hockey – that sort of thing."

"Well, you won't get a chance to do much of that around here," the chubby girl said. "I'm Andie Harrington. This is Eve Dedham."

Josie introduced herself. "What do you mean, I won't get a chance to play sports?"

"Not real team sports," Eve explained. "The only intramural sports we've got for girls here are tennis and gymnastics."

"You're kidding!" Josie was appalled. "Not even soccer?"

"Nope," Andie said. "Of course, that doesn't bother *me*." She grinned at Eve, who laughed. Then she explained to Josie, "I'm the only girl

26

in the history of Green Falls Junior High who almost failed phys. ed."

"Remember that time last year when you actually managed to make contact with a volley-ball?" Eve turned to Josie. "The whole class stopped playing and applauded."

Josie smiled thinly. She was still considering the disturbing information she'd just received. "The boys have team sports, don't they?"

"Oh, sure," Eve said. "Football, basketball, the usual stuff."

"Then how come there aren't any girls' sports?"

"I don't know," Andie said. "I've never thought about it."

Other girls had started to drift into the gym. "We better go in," Eve said. "Connors goes wild if you're late."

Josie followed them. "I don't see why we had to change our clothes," Andie grumbled. "You know we're just going to get Connors' annual speech on sportsmanship."

Great, Josie thought dismally. What was the need for a speech on sportsmanship if there weren't any sports?

The sign on the door read GREEN GAZETTE. Inside the room, Becka could see about a dozen kids, all gathered around a thin boy with wire-rimmed glasses. *He must be the editor*, Becka thought. She thought she recognised a few of the others from her classes.

Teachers had always told her she was a talented writer. What was a better place for a good writer than a newspaper? This might be the perfect extracurricular activity for her.

Still, she hesitated. The kids were all talking to each other, like they'd been together on the staff forever. She took a tentative step inside.

No one noticed her. No one called, "C'mon in, join us," or anything like that. The thought of just bursting into the group and announcing herself totally unnerved her. Clutching her books tightly, she turned around and walked back out into the hall. *You're such a chicken*, she scolded herself as she left the building and started towards home. Maybe after a few days, when kids got to know her, they'd invite her to join them in one activity or another. Then she'd feel more comfortable.

"How was the first day of school?" Annie asked as Becka walked into Morgan's Country Foods.

"Good," Becka said, placing her books on the counter. "I've got some really great teachers. Better than last year."

Annie looked pleased. "What about your classmates? Did you make some new friends?"

Becka paused. She didn't want Annie to think she was a social misfit. "Well, there's a nice girl in my English class. Louise. I don't think we have much in common, though."

"I'm sure you'll make lots of friends before long," Annie assured her.

Becka busied herself straightening some preserve jars on a shelf. "My English teacher's super. I think I'm going to *really* like that."

Josie entered the store in time to hear those last words. "You're going to really like what?"

"School," Becka replied.

Josie sniffed. "I'm not so sure I will."

"Why not?" Annie asked anxiously.

"There are no good sports for girls. And the girls' phys. ed. teacher is a real drip. We're doing aerobics! It's practically like dancing." She made a gagging sound.

"Oh, dear," Annie began, but she didn't get any farther. Cat burst in.

"Annie, can I go meet some kids at Brownies? I'll be back before dinner, I promise."

"Sure," Annie said. "In fact, you can all take off if you'd like." She looked around the empty store. "It doesn't look like I'm going to need any help here today."

"Great," Josie said. "I'm going over to the MacPhersons'. Red said some kids are coming over to shoot baskets in his driveway." She and Cat ran out.

"How about you, Becka?" Annie asked.

"I think I'll just stay here with you. We might get some customers."

Annie put an arm around her. "Honey, I know it can be hard to make friends at a new school. Why don't you catch up with Cat and go to Brownies with her?"

"No, really, I want to stay here," Becka insisted.

Annie still looked concerned, but just then the bell over the door jingled and a customer walked in. Annie went over to help her.

Becka could just imagine Cat's reaction if Becka announced she was going to Brownies with her. She hadn't even invited Becka to join her and her friends at lunch, and Becka felt pretty sure Cat had seen her sitting there alone.

But that didn't surprise her. Back at their old school, she'd never hung out with Cat. In fact, she'd never hung out with anyone. As long as she could remember, she'd been "one of the orphans," and no one ever paid much attention to her. Somehow, Cat had avoided that fate, but Becka had accepted it. That was just the way things were.

But it doesn't have to be like that here, she thought. She wasn't a pitiful orphan any more. She had a home and a family, just like everyone else. There were all those groups at school – there must be a place for her in one of them. She just had to figure out where she belonged and what she had to do to fit in.

Annie came back to the counter and rang up the purchase. As soon as the customer left, she turned to Becka. "Like I was saying, sweetie, it's easier for some people to make friends than it is for others. But that's what will be so nice about having two sisters in the same grade. Between the three of you, you'll have a huge circle of friends before long."

For Annie's benefit, Becka smiled brightly

and nodded. But she knew better. She certainly couldn't see herself shooting baskets with Josie and her friends. As for Cat, forget it. Cat wouldn't lift a finger to help Becka.

But that was okay, Becka decided. They probably wouldn't even like the same people. Becka would just figure out a way to make friends on her own. How hard could that be, anyway? If people didn't like her the way she was . . . well, she'd just be somebody else.

Three

Two days later, Becka lay on her bed reading a biography. It was about a woman named Anastasia, who claimed she was the daughter of the last czar of Russia. She was supposed to have been killed, along with other members of the royal family, but she said she had escaped. Some people didn't believe her; but others did. It was so very romantic.

The sun was going down, so she turned on the lamp. Finishing the last page, she closed the book and added it to the stack of biographies she'd taken out of the library. She wouldn't have to read them now. She knew this was the one she wanted to do her report on.

Then she went over to her desk and read her own autobiography for the third time. The punctuation and spelling were perfect. But after Anastasia's exciting life, it seemed awfully boring. And short. For thirteen years she'd lived in an orphanage. Then she was adopted. What else was there to write about?

Ms Levin had told them they should include interesting background on themselves, like about their parents and grandparents. But Becka didn't even know who her real parents were. She certainly didn't want to write that she'd been abandoned as a baby and left on the doorstep of Willoughby Hall. It was embarrassing, letting the teacher know her own parents hadn't wanted her. And what if she was one of the students chosen to read her essay aloud?

From downstairs, she heard Ben's voice calling up to her. "Becka! Come down and have some cookies!"

She stuck the assignment in her notebook and went down to the living room. At the bottom of the stairs, she paused for a minute. Scenes like this still sent waves of pleasure through her. At Willoughby Hall, you never knew who you'd find gathered together. Here, she knew she'd find her family. Always.

"The pep club is so cool! Everyone who's anyone belongs," Cat was saying.

"But what do they do?" Josie asked.

Cat waved an arm vaguely. "Oh, support the teams and all that. We're having a bake sale on Saturday to raise money for new basketball team uniforms."

The phone rang, and Becka wasn't surprised to see Cat jump up. It was always for her.

"Basketball uniforms," Josie echoed. "That figures. Everything's for the boys. I still can't believe there's no girls' basketball team."

"If you want a girls' basketball team, why don't you start one?" Becka suggested.

Cat returned. "That was Marla. She wanted

to know what I'm making for the bake sale. Annie, do you have any bright ideas?"

"Why don't you ask Josie?" Annie said. "She's the master baker."

Cat turned to Josie. "What should I make?"

Josie didn't reply. Her eyes were glazed over. Cat repeated her question.

"Uh, I don't know." Josie got up. "I'm going to make a phone call." She went back into the kitchen.

"Thanks," Cat said sarcastically. She turned to Ben.

"Ben, how's the room upstairs coming along?"

"Pretty good," he replied. "Have you girls decided who's going to get it?"

"Well, I had an idea," Cat said, curling up on the couch. "Becka's always complaining that I'm too messy. If I had my own room, I think she'd be a lot happier. Wouldn't you, Becka?"

Becka rolled her eyes as she took another cookie. Cat was so conniving. Luckily, Annie and Ben were starting to see through her.

"You could start being neater," Annie pointed out, her eyes twinkling. "I'm sure that would make Becka just as happy. Becka, are you involved in this bake sale, too?"

Becka shook her head. "I didn't join the pep club. I started to go to the meeting yesterday, but there were all these kids I didn't know. . . ."

"Cat would introduce you to people," Annie said. "Wouldn't you, Cat?"

Becka looked at Cat, who suddenly seemed

terribly interested in the cookie she was holding. She was spared having to answer when Josie bounded back into the room. "Becka, that was a brilliant idea!"

"What are you talking about?" Becka asked.

"Starting a basketball team! I just called Eve Dedham. She's on the tennis team, so I figured she'd know what I should do to get it started."

Cat looked up sharply. "Eve Dedham?"

"Yeah. You know her?"

"I know she's a friend of Heather Beaumont's."

"Who's Heather Beaumont?" Ben asked.

"Just the meanest girl in school." To Josie, Cat said, "If I were you, I wouldn't have anything to do with any friend of hers."

"Well, you're not me," Josie retorted.

"Now, Josie," Annie said. "Cat's just showing concern. Sisters *should* look out for each other."

Becka turned to hide a smile. Cat looking out for anyone but herself? What a joke.

"Well, I don't know Heather," Josie continued, "but Eve's okay. Anyway, she says she'll help me put up signs tomorrow, so all the girls interested in forming a team can meet."

"Sounds like an excellent idea," Ben said. He turned to Annie. "It looks like our girls are going to make a real impact on Green Falls Junior High."

Becka got up abruptly. "I have to go work on my assignment." She went back up to the bedroom and sat down on her bed. Cat and Josie might be making an impact. Becka was invisible. So far, the only person she'd even spoken to was Louise. And as nice as Louise was, Becka knew they wouldn't become close friends. Louise was a loner. Of course, so was Becka – but not by choice.

She had to think of a way to stand out, to make people notice her. Retrieving her assignment from her notebook, she read it again. Then she crumpled it up, went to her desk, and started over.

As the girls got out of the station wagon the next morning, Becka glanced at a group sitting on the steps. "Who are those kids?" There were about half a dozen boys and girls, all wearing black. One of the boys was in her homeroom, but she couldn't remember his name.

"Those are the greasers," Cat said. "They think they're really tough, and they're always getting into trouble, cutting class and stuff like that. They're real lowlifes."

"How do you know so much about them?" Josie asked.

"Everyone knows about them," Cat said airily. "Anyway, you can tell just by looking at them."

"You shouldn't judge a book by its cover," Becka told her. Actually, she thought they looked kind of interesting.

"I've got to go meet Eve," Josie said, and ran on into the school. Becka was still studying the group on the steps.

"Just stay away from them," Cat advised.

"Becka, are you really going to wear that hat to school?"

Becka touched the brim of her straw hat with a polka-dotted scarf dangling from it. "Sure. Why not?"

"Nobody wears hats," Cat informed her.

"*I* do," Becka replied.

"Do yourself a favour and take it off," Cat stated, and went into the school. Becka stared after her. Since when did she have to take orders from Cat? She looked at the kids on the steps again. At least they didn't look like they'd be snotty. She still had ten minutes before the homeroom bell.

"Excuse me, can I sit here?"

A boy with long, slicked-back hair glanced briefly at her. "It's a free country."

Becka took that as permission. She planted herself on the edge of a step.

"Cool hat," a girl commented.

Becka glowed. "Thank you."

"Hey, you guys hear about Nick?" One of the boys asked. "He got busted for shoplifting a cassette from the record store."

"What a jerk," another boy commented.

Becka nodded. "That sounds pretty stupid."

A girl grinned at her. "No kidding. Anyone who can't get out of a record store with a little cassette has to be seriously dumb."

Becka swallowed. That wasn't exactly what she had meant.

"I got out of a drugstore once with three

37

lipsticks and a bottle of shampoo," the girl announced proudly.

"Big deal," the other girl said. "I ripped off two pairs of shoes and a blouse from Harrison's Department Store." She turned to Becka. "You ever lifted anything?"

Becka thought. "I once walked out of a store with some shoelaces I hadn't paid for." She didn't add that it was a complete accident, and that she'd gone back the next day to pay for them.

No one looked very impressed. But at least they were talking to her. Becka looked at her watch. "It's almost time for the bell."

A boy shrugged. "No big deal. You can get three tardies before you have to stay for detention."

Becka rose. "Yeah, well, I've got two already, so I better go." Had she sounded convincingly tough?

She wasn't too sure this was the group for her. Of course, their attitude could be nothing but an act. They could all be lying about the shoplifting, just like she'd lied. And Cat didn't like them. That was a point in their favour.

Not to mention the fact that they weren't snobs. Maybe tomorrow she could borrow a black T-shirt from Josie. And she wouldn't wear any scarves or ribbons in her hair. It wouldn't be too hard to copy their look.

Becka spent homeroom reading over her new autobiography. If she was chosen to read aloud,

38

this would definitely make an impact. It wasn't easy to concentrate during her morning classes – she had to resist the urge to pull it out and read it again.

Finally, it was time for English. Louise looked up as she sat down. "When are the book reports due?"

"A week from tomorrow," Becka said. "What are you doing yours on?"

"I don't know," Louise said. "I went to the library, but all those biographies looked so boring."

"Want me to help you pick one out?" Becka asked.

Louise looked pleased. "Would you?"

"Sure. I'll meet you in the library after school." She stopped talking as Ms Levin came into the room.

"We're going to start right away reading our autobiographies aloud," she announced. "Do I have any volunteers?" Becka raised her hand, but Ms Levin picked a boy first.

Becka only half listened to the boy's report. She was too busy going over her own in her head. By now, she practically had it memorised. As soon as the boy finished, her hand shot up.

"Becka?"

Becka stood up and cleared her throat. "I grew up in an orphanage. I never knew my parents, but I believe that my background was something like this." She paused dramatically.

"My mother was a princess from a foreign country. While visiting the United States, she met a man who was an artist. He was very poor, and she was very rich, but they fell madly in love. Secretly, they got married. When my mother's parents found out, they were furious because they had arranged a marriage for her with a prince. Just after my mother gave birth to me, her family had her kidnapped and taken back to her own country. My father, being a poor artist, could not afford to feed me, so he brought me to the orphanage. This summer, I was adopted, and I love my new parents. But I know that somewhere, my real mother, who is now probably a queen, wonders what became of her beloved daughter."

There was a dead silence in the room when she finished. Becka had a feeling everyone was looking at her in a whole new way, seeing her for the first time.

"That was . . . interesting, Becka," Ms Levin said. "Very creative. Next?"

As the other kids read their autobiographies, Becka daydreamed about her future at Green Falls Junior High. If Cat was right, and Becka had to admit she usually was, word spread fast here. It wouldn't be long before everyone knew she might be a royal princess. She imagined herself surrounded by curious students, all begging her to join their groups.

When the bell rang, she closed her eyes and waited for the onslaught of attention.

"Becka? Are you feeling okay?"

She opened her eyes and looked at Louise. The two of them were the only ones left in class. "I'm fine."

"Well, see you in the library after school."

"Right." Becka got up and left the room. *Why didn't anyone speak to me about my autobiography,* she wondered. *Maybe they were just too overwhelmed.*

In the cafeteria, Becka got her tray and started towards the first empty table she saw. Then she saw some of the kids she'd sat with on the school steps.

She was so tired of sitting alone. . . .

"Your sister's sitting with the greasers," Marla whispered to Cat.

Cat turned to look. Sure enough, there was Becka at a table filled with lowlifes. She cringed.

"Who are you guys talking about?" Britt asked.

"Becka Morgan," Marla said.

"Oh yeah, she's in my English class." Britt grinned. "Get this. She claims she's the daughter of a royal princess. She said this, right in class! You should have seen everyone's expression. They all wanted to crack up. I had to put my hand over my mouth to keep from laughing out loud."

"Which one is she?" Trisha asked.

"The blonde sitting with the greasers," Britt told her. "The one with the silly hat." The significance of the last name appeared to have just hit her. "Cat, is she related to you?"

"Not really. She was adopted by the same people who adopted me."

"Then you're sisters?" Britt exclaimed.

"Just by accident," Cat said. "I don't think of us as sisters. I mean, look at her. She's a major dork." Quickly, she changed the subject. "What are you guys making for the bake sale?"

As the girls began to discuss their contributions, Cat poked at her food. Why was she suddenly so uncomfortable putting Becka down like that? Back at Willoughby Hall, she was always making fun of her.

"How about you, Cat?"

"Huh?"

"What are you making for the bake sale?"

"Gee, I don't know." Cat's eyes drifted around the room and settled on Todd and Heather. "I suppose Heather will be making something extraordinary."

"Heather!" Trisha snorted. "She wouldn't dirty her hands in the kitchen. I heard her say she's ordering something from a bakery. Eclairs, I think."

"I wish I knew what Todd's favourite food is," Cat murmured.

"I can tell you that," Britt announced. "When we were little kids, I used to go to his birthday parties. And instead of a cake, he always had a blueberry pie." She giggled. "I remember because the candles always sank into the filling."

"Blueberry pie," Cat mused. "Very interesting."

Heading for the door after lunch with the others, Cat saw Becka dropping off her tray on the conveyor belt. "I'll see you guys later," she said to her friends, and strode purposefully towards Becka.

"Becka, I just heard about what you said in English class today."

Becka actually looked pleased. "Really? What were people saying?"

"Not much. Mainly, they were laughing at you."

Becka's lower lip started trembling, and Cat almost felt sorry for her. But when she spoke, she made her voice harsh. "Honestly, Becka, how can you be so goofy? Did you really think people were going to believe you're a princess? I wouldn't care except for the fact that we have the same last name." She caught herself. Was she being too cruel? No, it was probably the only way to get through to her.

At least Becka's lips stopped trembling. Now they were pressed together in a tight line. She said, "I don't believe you."

"Well, it's true," Cat retorted. "And what were you doing with those greasers? I *told* you they have a bad reputation. You want everyone to think you're a gangster, too?" She would have gone on, but she was startled by the glint in Becka's eyes. She couldn't remember ever seeing an expression like that on Becka's face before. She almost looked angry!

And her tone was steely. "Just because you don't like them doesn't mean I can't." With that, Becka turned and walked away.

Cat shook her head in exasperation. Then she noticed a sign on the cafeteria wall: *Attention: all girls interested in forming a basketball team. Come to a meeting after school today in room C-301. Or call Josie Morgan.* This was followed by the Morgans' home phone number.

Silently, Cat groaned. There was *another* Morgan making a fool out of herself. Were the two of them in a conspiracy to make her feel embarrassed? Cat was going to have to be awfully cool to live down the two of them.

Remembering her promise to Louise, Becka headed for the library after her last class. Even though it had been three hours since her little run-in with Cat, she was still burning. Back at Willoughby Hall, Cat had always been making fun of her. Becka had thought it would be different now that they were family. Obviously, she was wrong.

How dare Cat lie like that, saying kids were laughing at her? And she had no business telling Becka who she could be friends with.

Louise was waiting for her in the library, or "media centre," as the name on the door indicated. It was a cheerful, modern room, much bigger than the one back at her old school.

A pretty woman with long curly hair approached them. "Can I help you girls find something?"

"Biographies," Louise said glumly.

"I know where they are," Becka said.

The woman smiled at her. "Yes, I've seen you in here several times this week. What's your name?"

"Becka Morgan. I'm new this year."

"I'm Ms Lesser, the librarian. How do you like our media centre?"

"It's super," Becka said. "What's that over there?" She pointed to a separate, glassed-in room where several kids were.

"That's where we keep record albums and cassettes," Ms Lesser said. "It's soundproof, so students can listen to music without bothering anyone." She smiled in amusement. "Unfortunately, they also use it for other purposes."

Becka saw what she meant. Even though she couldn't hear them, she could see that they were talking and laughing. They looked like they were having fun, though. Then she realised one of them was Cat.

She turned away. "Come on," she said to Louise. "I'll help you pick out a book."

"I guess it'll have to be about someone like George Washington or Thomas Jefferson," Louise sighed. "Those are the kind of people who get biographies written about them."

"They're not the only ones," Becka said. "I'll find someone you'll think is interesting." She began searching the shelves. Then she grabbed a book and pulled it out. "Here."

Louise read the cover. "Elizabeth Blackwell. Never heard of her."

"Well, you should," Becka said. "She was the first woman doctor."

"You're kidding!" Louise's expression changed. She almost looked enthusiastic. "Hey, this might not be so bad. Thanks, Becka."

"You're welcome." Becka glanced back at the soundproof room.

"Who are you looking at?" Louise asked. "Do you know them?"

"Just the girl with the black hair."

"What's so special about her?"

"She's my sister. Well, sort of. We were adopted by the same family."

"Oh. She's pretty."

"Yeah." Becka sighed. "We're different."

"I've got an older brother," Louise said, "and we're really different, too. He's in high school. He's already started his own business."

"What kind of business?"

"He has this group of high school kids who dress up and entertain at parties. Like, you can hire someone to dress up as Santa Claus for a Christmas party. Or just go to someone's house with a bunch of balloons and sing "Happy Birthday." The hospital hired them once to come over dressed as rabbits for an Easter party in the children's ward."

Becka sure couldn't picture serious Louise doing anything like that. So blood siblings weren't any more alike than adopted ones. But learning that didn't lift her spirits.

Watching Cat and those kids together made her feel lonely. "Hey, Louise, want to go to Main Street? We could get an ice cream or something."

"Gee, I'd like to, but I can't. I'm a candy striper at the hospital and I have to be there in twenty minutes."

"What's a candy striper?"

"We do volunteer work. You know, read to kids, run errands, that sort of thing. You could sign up to do it if you'd like."

Becka smiled politely. But she knew she wouldn't. She'd always been squeamish about seeing blood or people in pain. Being a candy striper wasn't for her.

She left the library with Louise and walked with her to the exit. But she didn't leave. For some reason, the thought of going straight home, like she did every day, bothered her. She could always go back to the library, but then she'd have to see Cat, with all her new friends.

A sign by the door caught her eye – It was for Josie's basketball meeting. Maybe she'd just run upstairs and see how it was going.

Becka expected to see a whole crowd of

athletic girls in room 301. Instead, there were only Josie and one other girl. "Is the meeting over already?" Becka asked.

Josie's face was bleak. "There wasn't any meeting. No one showed up."

"It's a shame," the other girl said. "I guess there just aren't any girls here who want to play basketball."

"Except me," Josie said mournfully. "Oh, Eve, this is Becka. Becka, Eve."

"Do you play basketball, too?" Becka asked.

"No, I'm on the tennis team, and I don't have time for any other sports."

"At least you've got tennis," Josie said. "I won't be playing real basketball again till high school. I hope they have a girls' team *there*."

"Why are there separate boys' and girls' teams, anyway?" Becka asked. "It's the same game, isn't it?"

"There are a few different rules," Josie said. "But yeah, it's basically the same game."

Becka didn't know anything about basketball, except for the fact that the players were tall. "Then why can't you just be on the boys' team? You're as tall as most of the eighth-grade boys."

Josie's mouth fell open, and Becka took an involuntary step backward. Was she going to call her an idiot, like Cat?

"Becka, you're a genius!" Josie turned to Eve excitedly. "What do you think? Would they ever let girls on a boys' team?"

"I don't know," Eve said. "Let's go back to my house and ask my brother. He's in high school, but he used to play basketball here. He knows Coach Meadows really well."

The girls started towards the door. "Becka, tell Annie and Ben where I went, okay?"

"Sure," Becka said. She stood there alone in the room for a minute. Then she left and slowly made her way down the stairs towards the exit.

There were still some kids hanging around in front of the school. One of them actually spoke to her. "Hey! You want to come with us?"

It was one of the girls she'd sat with at lunch. She was sitting on the steps with two of the other so-called greasers.

"Where are you going?" Becka asked.

"Over to Nick's to get some spray paint," she said. "We're going to sneak back into the school, and spray stuff on the cheerleaders' lockers."

Becka was confused. "What are you doing that for?"

The girl shrugged. "Just for kicks."

Graffiti on lockers? That wasn't her style. Becka shook her head. "No, thanks." Sadly, she watched them amble away. So they weren't just pretending to be bad kids. They really were. Cat was right.

Becka could have gotten into this group. But she just wasn't a lawbreaker, and there was no way she could fake that. *Well, I'll just find another group*, Becka told herself.

The exit door swung open and two boys burst

49

out, colliding with Becka. "Ow!" Becka cried out.

The boys stopped. Becka recognised one of them from English. "Excuse me," he said. Then he looked her in the face and grinned in a not-very-nice way. "Your Highness." He bowed.

"Better watch out," the other boy said to him. "She might order your head cut off." They both started laughing like hyenas before running off.

Becka shrank back against the wall. A great big lump was forming in her throat. Did Cat *always* have to be right? The thought was discouraging.

And infuriating.

Four

Early Saturday morning, Cat leaned against the kitchen counter and read the directions for piecrust from the open cookbook propped in front of her. Sunlight was streaming in from the windows of the country kitchen, but Cat was totally unaware of it. She was concentrating.

She measured out the flour, sugar, and butter, and tossed them into a bowl. So far, this was easy. She studied the list of ingredients again. Two egg yolks. She frowned.

"What's wrong?" Annie asked, walking in.

"It says here I have to put in two egg yolks. How am I supposed to get just the yolk in and not the rest of the egg?"

"That's something I never got the hang of," Annie said. "I've seen people do it. You break the shell and slide the egg back and forth till all that's left is the yolk. Every time I tried it, the yolk broke. What are you making?"

"A blueberry pie for the pep club bake sale," Cat told her.

Annie's face was doubtful. "That's a pretty ambitious undertaking, if you've never done much baking. I'd help you, but I'm afraid I don't have much experience with pies. Why don't you ask Josie to help?"

Cat shook her head. "I can handle it," she stated, with more confidence than she felt.

"Well, okay. I'm going out to pick some flowers." Annie left, and Cat pulled a bowl of fresh eggs from the refrigerator. Selecting one, she tapped it gently against the side of the bowl. The shell cracked, and before Cat could start rocking it, the entire egg dropped into the flour mixture. Frantically, Cat tried to get the white out with a spoon, but a lot of flour came with it and she couldn't tell if she got all the white stuff.

With the next egg, Cat broke it into a separate bowl and tried to spoon out the yolk. But the yellow blob broke and she couldn't get it on the spoon. She got as much as she could into the big bowl. After all, how much harm could a little white do, anyway?

Cat checked the instructions again and grimaced. Gritting her teeth, she plunged her hands into the gooey mess and started mashing it all together. The stuff oozed between her fingers and collected under her nails. It felt disgusting.

"You're working that dough too hard," came Josie's voice from behind her.

"Mind your own business," Cat snapped irritably. With her arm, she wiped a bead of sweat from her forehead.

"Suit yourself," Josie said. "But it won't be

flaky. When you work the dough like that, the crust comes out soggy."

Cat peered down into the goo. She pictured Todd's expression when he bit into a soggy slice of pie. She heard the laughter of Heather and her friends. It was time to put pride aside.

She bestowed her sweetest smile on Josie. "Could you help me with it?"

Josie smirked. "I thought I was supposed to mind my own business."

"Please?" Cat wheedled.

She should have known Josie would enjoy having her in a humble position. Josie took her time considering the request. Luckily, Ben walked in, and Cat took advantage of his presence to repeat her plea. "Oh, Josie, I really need you. You're such a fabulous cook. Couldn't you help me?"

"All right," Josie said. "The sale's for basketball uniforms, right? It's a good cause." She emptied the contents of Cat's bowl into the wastebasket.

"That's a switch," Ben said. "I thought you were down on boys' sports."

"I can't be anymore," Josie replied, grinning. "Since I can't get a girls' basketball team started, I'm going to see if I can try out for the boys' team."

Cat looked at her in horror. "You're going to play basketball with *boys*?"

"If the coach lets me," Josie said, as she deftly cut butter into the flour and sugar mixture.

"That's a great idea!" Ben said enthusiastically. "I've never understood why junior high sports have to be separated by sex. At your age, boys and girls are about the same size, right?"

"I'm taller than most of the boys in my classes," Josie agreed. "I just hope this Coach Meadows is as open-minded as you are."

"What are you guys talking about?" Annie said, returning from the backyard with an armful of flowers.

"Josie's going to try out for the boys' basketball team," Ben told her.

"Terrific!" Annie exclaimed. "Like they say: if you can't beat 'em, join 'em."

Cat couldn't understand their enthusiasm. Didn't they see how ridiculous Josie would look, the only girl on a boys' team? The boys would make fun of her, and the girls would be grossed out by her. Josie could end up being the laughing stock of Green Falls Junior High. And by then, everyone was bound to know Josie was Cat's sister. Maybe she could be talked out of it.

Ben left to open the store, and Annie went into the dining room with the flowers. Cat lingered in the kitchen, trying to think of something to say about this basketball business. But before she could, Josie said, "Don't you have something else to do? I don't mean to be rude, but I can't work with you looking over my shoulder."

Maybe this wasn't the right time to criticise

Josie's plans, Cat thought. Not when she needed a great pie for the bake sale.

In the dining room, Annie was arranging the flowers in a vase. "Where's Becka?" she asked.

"Up in the bedroom, reading," Cat replied.

Annie's forehead creased. "She's been spending a lot of time alone lately."

"She likes being alone," Cat said.

Annie didn't look convinced. "Sometimes, maybe. But I think she's lonely. Cat, see if you can talk her into going to that bake sale today."

"Okay." Cat went upstairs and found Becka in the same position she'd last seen her in – lying on her bed, a book propped on her stomach.

"Are you coming to the bake sale?" Cat asked.

Becka's eyes lit up. "Can I?"

Cat shrugged. "Sure. Anyone can go." The light went out of Becka's eyes, and she returned to her book.

Cat turned away. She knew what Becka wanted. She was hoping for an invitation to join Cat and her friends. Quickly, Cat fabricated an excuse. "I have to be there early, to help set up. Only pep club members can do that."

Becka turned a page and didn't say anything. For a split second, a wave of pity passed through Cat. She fought it back. Why should she feel sorry for Becka? It was Becka's own fault she didn't have any friends. What else could she expect when she went around saying dumb things and wearing goofy clothes?

Cat picked up a hairbrush and ran it through her hair. "You really should go. It's a chance to meet some people."

"Maybe I will," Becka said. "But don't worry. If I run into you, I won't say anything in front of your friends. You can just pretend you don't know me."

Cat's hand faltered in her brushing rhythm. Then she pressed her lips together tightly and brushed harder. Becka's problems weren't *her* problems. She wasn't about to feel guilty about them.

Tables laden with every imaginable kind of cake, pie, pastry, and cookie had been set up in the parking lot beside the school. Helium-filled balloons in the school colours, blue and yellow, added a festive air. Signs proclaimed the contributions of the pep club members – "Andy's Famous Brownies," "Carrie's Carrot Cake," and so on.

Wandering around by herself, Becka recognised a number of kids from her classes. She even knew some of their names by now. But there was no one she felt comfortable approaching and striking up a conversation with.

She seemed to be the only person there walking alone. If only she'd been able to talk Louise into coming. But Louise did her volunteer work at the hospital on Saturdays, and she wasn't going to give that up to come to a bake sale.

Becka didn't see any of the greasers there, either. Not that she missed them. They weren't her kind of people. But at least they *talked* to her.

When she realised she was approaching Cat's table, she quickened her step. Out of the corner of her eye, she saw Marla, Cat's friend. Of course, Cat had never bothered to introduce Becka to Marla. Becka only knew her name because she'd asked Cat.

Marla actually smiled at her as she passed, but Becka kept her eyes straight ahead. If Cat didn't want Becka to know her friends, so be it. There were two kids from Becka's English class with them, too – Todd, the football and basketball captain, and Britt. They were all laughing and having a great time.

Then she saw Josie with Red MacPherson and Eve, the girl who had helped Josie organise her basketball meeting. A couple of other kids were with them, too. Josie beckoned her over.

"Becka, this is Andie Harrington and Jason Wister. Jason's the editor of the *Green Gazette*, and he says if I try out for the basketball team, he'll write an article about it!"

"That's nice," Becka said. She was more interested in hearing that Jason was the newspaper editor. Maybe she could ask him about joining the staff. But that might sound pushy. Before she could make up her mind, Eve began talking about the tennis team.

"I hope you send a reporter to cover our next game," she said to Jason. "You hardly ever give us any attention at all!"

Jason grinned. "Hey, I don't have all that much space, you know. And there are a lot of sports to cover."

"Speaking of sports," Red said, "I went to a lacrosse game at the high school last spring. It was really cool."

"I don't even know what that is," Andie said. Red started explaining the game and Becka's attention wandered. She saw a girl with long blonde hair coming towards them.

"Eve," the girl called. "Come help me arrange my pastries." Her voice had the sound of someone who was accustomed to having her commands obeyed.

"I'm coming, Heather," Eve called back. To the others, she said, "See you later," and took off.

Andie grimaced. "Eve always jumps the minute Heather Beaumont opens her mouth."

"Heather's the one Cat doesn't like," Josie told Becka.

Looking at Heather, Becka could understand why. She was really beautiful. Cat didn't like competition in that department.

"It looks like Heather's giving Cat the evil eye," Red remarked.

"That's because Cat's talking to Todd Murphy," Andie reported. "Heather considers Todd to be her own exclusive property."

"How do you know all this?" Jason asked.

Andie grinned. "I hear everything that goes on in this school. Hey, Jason, why don't you let me do a gossip column for the newspaper? I know all kinds of dirt."

Jason looked at her in mock horror. "A gossip column in *my* newspaper? Forget it!" He turned to Josie. "But you let me know if Coach Meadows gives you a chance to try out for the basketball team. If he doesn't, I'll do a major editorial."

"Oh, I don't think she'll have any problem trying out," Red said. "Coach Meadows is pretty cool."

They were talking sports again, and Becka felt excluded. She moved away, pretty sure that none of them would miss her. She started wandering around again, not even knowing where she was going, just drifting aimlessly. Then she found herself at the table right next to Cat's.

Cat's back was to her, and she was still talking to Todd. Becka couldn't help overhearing the conversation.

"Who made the blueberry pie?" he was asking Cat.

"I did. Would you like a slice?"

"I'm going to buy the whole pie," Todd replied. "I'm crazy about blueberry pie. It's my favourite."

"You're kidding!" Cat exclaimed. "That's amazing. Just this morning, I was trying to decide what to bake. Something kept telling me blueberry pie."

Todd grinned. "Hey, maybe it was – what do you call it? – ESP or something." He looked around the parking lot. "This was a great idea. I hope you make a lot of money. We sure can use some new uniforms."

"Oh, that's right, you're on the basketball team."

"Yeah. I'm captain this year."

Becka didn't have to be able to see Cat's face to know what her reaction would be. "Captain! How fabulous!" Cat gushed. "How's the team?"

"Not bad. Hey, get this. Red MacPherson told me there's a girl who wants to try out. What was her name? Joanie?"

There was a moment of silence, then Becka heard Cat say, "Josie."

"You know her?"

"Actually, she's my . . . well, she was adopted by the same people who adopted me." After a pause, her next words came out in a rush. "It's *so* embarrassing. Imagine, a girl on a boys' team."

"Wouldn't bother me," Todd said. "If she's any good."

"I think it's silly," Cat continued. "But Josie's strange. She's not very feminine. Sometimes I think she'd rather be a boy than a girl."

Becka was appalled. How could Cat talk like that? Didn't she have any family loyalty? Not only was she saying nasty things about Josie, she could be ruining her chances of getting on the team by talking to the captain like this.

"Wow, you guys must be really different," Todd remarked.

"Oh, we are," Cat assured him. "And then there's the other one, Becka." She sighed deeply.

"Oh yeah, she's in my English class. She's the one who thinks she's a princess."

Cat giggled. She spoke in a low voice, but not so low that Becka couldn't hear. "Do they have princesses on Mars? She's such a little space cadet. Totally out of it."

Becka's entire body was hot, and her face was burning. Her fists were clenched so hard her knuckles were white. Dimly, she was aware of Jason, the newspaper editor, passing by with a camera in his hand. He paused by Cat and Todd.

"I want to get some photos for the newspaper," he announced.

Cat immediately picked up her pie and smiled prettily. Jason considered her pose and shook his head. "I want something different, with action. Hey, Becka!"

Cat turned in alarm, surprised to see Becka so close by. Still steaming with rage, Becka managed to keep a placid face as she looked up. "What?"

"Come be in a picture."

Like a robot, Becka made her way stiffly towards him. Cat's friends Marla and Britt came over to watch, and some other kids gathered around. Becka noticed Heather among them. She could appreciate the way Heather was looking at Cat. It captured what Becka was feeling towards her, too.

Jason took the pie from Cat's hands and held it out to Becka. "Take this and hold it up, like you're about to throw it at Cat."

"But be careful!" Todd interjected. "I'm gonna buy that pie!"

Becka took the pie and faced Cat, who still had that fake sweeter-than-sugar smile on her face. She held up the pie and had a fleeting image of actually hitting Cat with it. If only she had the guts!

"Perfect," Jason said. He aimed his camera at them. "Now, smile!"

Becka wasn't sure she'd be able to do that. But she didn't even have time to try – from behind her, she felt a hard shove. And the arm holding the pie was propelled forward, in the direction of Cat.

It all happened so fast that it didn't even seem real. The flash from the camera bulb made it seem even less real. But there was Cat, with blueberry pie all over her face and dripping down onto her white sundress.

For a moment, everyone was too stunned to speak. Cat recovered first. "Becka!" she shrieked.

Marla grabbed a bunch of napkins and gave them to Cat, who started wiping her face. "Oh, no!" Cat screamed. "Look at my dress!"

"Oh, I'm *so* sorry." Heather Beaumont stepped out from behind Becka. "I bumped into her. I guess I just wasn't looking where I was going."

The fury blazing from Cat's eyes shifted from Becka to Heather, but Becka couldn't miss the fire. Then, with as much dignity as anyone who was covered with blueberry pie could muster, Cat strode off in the direction of the school. Britt ran after her and Marla followed, but not before giving Heather a particularly disgusted look.

Becka was still in a state of shock. Todd looked slightly stunned, too, but he managed a nervous smile at Heather. She ignored him and turned her attention to Becka.

"Oh dear, some of that pie got on you."

Becka looked down. There were small blue splatters on her shirt.

"I've got a sweater in my locker," Heather said. "Come with me, and I'll lend it to you. I'm so *very* sorry about this. I hope your shirt isn't ruined."

She sounded sincere, and friendlier than anyone had been to her yet at Green Falls Junior High. She put an arm around Becka and led her towards the school. "You're Cat Morgan's sister, aren't you?"

"Yes," Becka said. Then, remembering how Cat had described *her*, she amended that. "Not really, though. We were just adopted by the same people."

Heather gave her a sympathetic smile. "You don't sound like you're the best of friends."

"We're not," Becka said. Cat's words were still ringing in her ears.

Heather's smile widened. "I understand. Sisters can be such a pain."

"No kidding," Becka said with feeling. "Well, Josie's okay, but Cat . . ." She couldn't even come up with the right words to describe Cat.

Heather seemed to understand without any explanation. "You know, I really am sorry I bumped into you. But you have to admit, Cat looked pretty funny."

A clear image of Cat formed in Becka's mind. Miss Perfect, Miss Popularity, Miss I Don't Care About Anyone But Myself, with her pretty face and shiny hair and immaculate dress covered with blueberry pie. Becka's mouth twitched. *Stop that*, she warned herself. *It's mean and cruel to make fun of someone else's misfortune.*

But she remembered what Cat had said about her and Josie. She didn't deserve any sympathy. Becka couldn't help herself. She burst out laughing.

Heather joined in. They laughed together all the way into the school. Becka had to admit it felt wonderful – not just to be able to laugh at Cat. But to have someone to laugh with.

Five

On Monday morning, clutching a paper bag, Becka manoeuvred through the groups crowding the hall before the homeroom bell. She peered down the row of lockers that lined the wall.

Heather wasn't there yet. Nervously, Becka smoothed the pleats of her plain, navy blue skirt and fingered the buttons of her blouse with matching navy stripes. A smile briefly crossed her face as she recalled Annie's surprise when she picked out this outfit during their shopping expedition the day before. Annie knew very well this wasn't Becka's style.

Cat was surprised, too, though she gave grudging approval to Becka's new conservative look. She even offered the loan of a matching headband. *That* surprised Becka. She'd expected more hostility from Cat after the pie incident on Saturday. But Cat seemed to accept that it really had been an accident on Becka's part.

Becka caught her breath. She could see Heather coming from the opposite end of the hall with another girl. Both wore pleated skirts and blouses. Again, Becka touched her own skirt. Yes, she was absolutely right to wear this outfit. Even if it did feel stiff and unnatural.

She made her way down the hall to where Heather and her friend stood by Heather's open locker. The other girl saw her first. Her eyes swept over Becka, and her lips curled into a sneer. That wasn't very encouraging, but Becka steeled herself and coughed.

"Hi, Heather."

Heather whirled around and faced her. To Becka's relief, a big smile appeared. "Hi, Becka."

Becka held up the bag. "I brought your sweater back. The one you lent me."

"Thank you! You didn't need to bring it back so soon."

The other girl giggled. "She didn't need to bring it back at all. You've got so many sweaters, you wouldn't have missed it."

"Oh, I wouldn't have *kept* it," Becka said. "I mean, it's *yours*."

The girl Becka didn't know sneered again. Becka noticed that her hair was cut and styled exactly like Heather's. It was limp, though, and didn't look nearly as nice. She had awfully small eyes, too, not big ones like Heather's. And they were glaring at Becka as if she were some kind of dangerous intruder. Becka plunged ahead.

"I'm Becka," she said. The girl gave her a look that clearly said, "Who cares?"

"Becka *Morgan*," Heather said. She poked

the other girl. "Cat's sister. Becka, this is Blair Chase."

"Nice to meet you," Becka said.

Blair's mouth stretched into something that vaguely resembled a smile. Then her eyes moved beyond Becka. "Look who's coming."

Todd Murphy was heading towards them. "Hi, Heather," he said, sounding nervous.

Heather gave him a look through narrowed eyes. Then she twirled around and slammed her locker door with more force than necessary. Todd stood there awkwardly for another few seconds. When it became apparent that Heather wasn't going to speak to him, he slinked away.

"Wow," Blair commented. "You really shot him down."

"He deserves it," Heather stated. "He can't flirt with other girls and expect me to take it."

"But he's so cute," Blair said. "Are you sure you want to break up with him?"

"Oh, we're not breaking up. I just want him to suffer for a while before I take him back."

Poor Todd, Becka thought. Still, she admired Heather's confidence. She was even more sure of herself than Cat.

Heather and Blair continued to discuss Todd, and Becka figured they'd forgotten she was there. "Uh, I guess I'll get to homeroom."

Heather flashed a smile at her. "Come sit with us at lunch today, okay?"

Becka was dumbstruck. Finally, she managed

to stammer, "Okay." Then she floated all the way to her homeroom. As soon as she got there, she hurried over to Louise.

"Do you know Heather Beaumont?"

"Sure," Louise said. "I mean, I know who she *is*. She's a real big shot. Cheerleading captain and all that. Why?"

Becka felt like she was radiating joy. "She invited me to sit with her at lunch."

Louise seemed impressed. And surprised. "Really? She always seemed like such a snob. She must think you're somebody special."

All morning long, Louise's words rang in Becka's ears. *Somebody special.* One of the most important girls at school thought she was somebody special. She, Becka Morgan. Former nobody. Former orphan.

On the way to her next class, Becka saw Josie and ran up to her.

"Guess what? Heather Beaumont asked me to sit with her at lunch!"

"That's nice," Josie replied vaguely.

"Did you hear what I said? *Heather Beaumont.*"

"Yeah." Josie didn't appear terribly interested. But at least she explained why. "I'm on my way to see Coach Meadows. I'm a little nervous."

Becka patted Josie comfortingly on the shoulder. "You'll do great," she said with feeling.

"Thanks," Josie said. "I better run. I don't want to be late."

"Good luck!" Becka called after her. She didn't mind when a couple of passing kids turned and looked at her oddly. She wanted Josie to feel just as special and wanted as she did.

The office door was open, and Josie could see a large man sitting behind a desk, grading papers. The big silver whistle hanging from a chain around his neck identified him. Josie rapped lightly.

"Come in," he said without looking up.

"Uh, Coach Meadows?"

"Yes."

"I'm . . . I'm Josie Morgan. I wanted to talk to you."

"Speak up, young lady," he barked.

"I'm Josie Morgan –"

"I heard that," the man said. "What do you want?"

Josie had prepared a whole speech. But the man's gruff voice seemed to blow it right out of her head. "I . . . I want to play basketball," she blurted out.

The coach's unblinking eyes met hers. "Who's stopping you?"

Josie wished he didn't look quite so fierce. This was worse than facing Mrs Scanlon back at Willoughby Hall with dirty fingernails. "Well, there's no girls' basketball here. So I was wondering if I can, well you know . . ."

"If you can *what*?" he bellowed.

69

"If I can try out for the team!" Josie shouted. Then she clapped a hand over her mouth. Had she really yelled at the coach?

But he didn't seem to mind. He looked at her thoughtfully. "You ever play before?"

"In my phys. ed. class at my old school," Josie said. "And I shoot baskets a lot. I think I'm pretty good."

Coach Meadows grunted. "We'll see about that. Meet me in the gym after the last bell."

Josie wasn't sure she'd heard correctly. "You're going to let me try out?"

"That's what you want, isn't it?"

Josie nodded.

"Anything else?"

Josie shook her head.

The coach turned back to the papers on his desk. Josie fled.

Cat couldn't believe her eyes. She blinked twice. Then she leaned across the cafeteria table. "Marla, am I seeing what I think I'm seeing? Check out Heather's table."

Marla squinted. Then she raised her eyebrows. "Is that Becka?"

Britt was surprised, too. "What's she doing sitting with *them*?"

"Doesn't she know how you feel about Heather?" Marla asked.

"I think so," Cat said. She was truly puzzled. "What I can't figure out is why *they'd* want *her* around."

"That's not a very nice thing to say about your sister," Sharon said reprovingly.

Cat sighed. "If you knew Becka, you'd understand what I mean. She's not their type."

"Did those blueberry stains come out of your dress?" Marla asked.

"No. And it was practically brand-new." Cat grimaced at the memory. "I ought to make Heather pay for it."

"Do you really think she pushed Becka on purpose?" Britt asked.

"Of course she did. She saw me talking to Todd, and she wanted to get back at me."

"It sounds like something Heather would do," Marla remarked. "She always gets even."

"I suppose now she thinks I'll stay away from Todd," Cat mused.

"I think that was the general idea," Marla said.

Cat sneaked another quick peek at Heather. She was accustomed to being envied. Even when she was an orphan, no one ever felt sorry for her. She was too pretty and too popular to be pitied. She figured there would always be girls who didn't appreciate the fact that she could attract just about any boy she wanted. However, she'd never come across one as formidable as Heather.

But Cat was no wimp. "Well, I don't scare that easily. In fact, Todd just asked me to go to Brownies with him after school. And I said yes."

"I wouldn't let that get around if I were you," Marla cautioned her. "Heather holds a grudge."

Cat brushed that away. "What's she going to do? Throw a pie at me every time I talk to Todd?"

"No, but she's pretty sneaky," Marla told her. "Just be careful. And warn your sisters about her."

"Why?"

"Well, she might try to get back at you through them."

Cat laughed. "That's silly. *They're* not my problem, anyway." She turned to look again at the other table and decided to let Heather know what she was up against. "I'll be right back."

Cat got up and went over to Heather's table. Totally ignoring the other girls, Cat directed her words to Becka. "When you get home, tell Annie I went to Brownies with Todd, okay?"

Without waiting for a reply, she sauntered away.

"That was really nasty," Eve murmured.

Blair agreed. "She's got some nerve."

Heather didn't say anything, but her lips were pressed together so tightly they were white.

Becka was aghast at Cat's rude behaviour. She wondered if she should apologise for her. After all, they were related, sort of.

"Cat's not very tactful sometimes," she began tentatively.

"That's putting it mildly." Heather snorted.

She looked at Becka, her eyes awash with sympathy. "You poor thing. You have to live with her."

Becka marvelled at Heather's sensitivity. "It's difficult, sometimes," she admitted.

"Do you two get along?" Eve asked.

"Not . . . not all the time."

Heather leaned forward and spoke in a quiet, confidential tone. "What's she *really* like?"

Becka hesitated. Despite her general annoyance with Cat, she felt funny about reporting Cat's generally obnoxious behaviour to girls she hardly knew. There was family loyalty and all that to consider.

But remembering the cruel words Cat had used about *her*, Becka wondered if she should care about family loyalty. Cat didn't. Not to mention the fact that Becka had taken Cat's insults for thirteen years at Willoughby Hall.

"Could you excuse me for a minute? I'm going to get some more water."

The fountain was right by the table where Cat and her friends were sitting. As Becka filled her glass, she glanced at them. Cat was looking straight at her. Her eyes were baleful.

Then it hit her. Cat was jealous! Here Becka was, sitting with some of the most important girls at school, and Cat envied her.

A thrill shot through Becka. All her life, she'd envied Cat – her confidence, her looks, her popularity. Now the roles were reversed.

It serves her right, Becka thought, especially

after calling her a pitiful wimp, refusing to introduce Becka to her friends, acting like she was ashamed – not just of her, but Josie, too. Becka met Cat's eyes evenly. Then, with a new determination, she marched back to Heather's table, ready to answer Heather's question.

"Cat's always been selfish and conceited. She's a major phony. She'll do anything to get what she wants. She doesn't care who she hurts. She uses people. And she lies, too, all the time." Even as the words poured out of her, she felt uncomfortable. Then she reminded herself how mean Cat had always been, and hardened her heart.

"How awful for you!" Heather exclaimed.

"It's better now that we're adopted," Becka continued. "I don't think Annie and Ben will let her get away with the kind of things she got away with at the orphanage."

"Does Josie get along with her?" Eve asked.

"Josie doesn't pay much attention to her. She's so caught up in this basketball thing."

"What basketball thing?" Heather asked quickly.

Eve explained. "She's trying out for the basketball team. I think she's got a good chance of making it, too."

Blair turned to Heather. "Isn't Todd captain this year?"

"Yes, he is," Heather said thoughtfully. Then her face grew sad. "But let's not talk about Todd, okay? I'll just get depressed. I can't

74

believe he's taking her to Brownies. That's always been *our* place."

"You know you can always get him back," Blair said.

"Mmm. But I want to know what's really going on between him and Cat." Heather turned her charming smile on Becka. "How would you like to be my spy?"

Becka blinked. "Your spy?"

"Yes! You could let me know what Cat and Todd are up to."

Becka bit her lip. This sounded kind of creepy. But Heather looked so anxious. "Please, Becka? I'd be so grateful. And this is the kind of thing friends do for each other."

Friends. What a beautiful word. Heather was calling her a friend. That was a lot more than Cat had been to her. Maybe she could do this for a little while, as a favour to Heather.

Becka nodded. "Okay. I'll be a regular Mata Hari."

"A what?" Heather asked.

"Mata Hari. She was a famous spy, a long time ago." Becka frowned. "Of course, she was caught. And executed. By a firing squad."

Heather reached over and patted her hand. "Don't worry. We don't have firing squads at Green Falls Junior High."

Blair and Eve started laughing, and Becka joined in. This was wonderful, just what she'd dreamed about – being part of a group, talking and laughing. All she had to do was mould herself into the image of the group and she'd fit right in.

Dressed in her phys. ed. uniform, Josie made her way out of the girls' locker room and into the gym. This was it, the moment she'd been waiting for. She rubbed the tiny ruby on her ring finger for good luck.

Sitting on the bleachers were Coach Meadows and a boy Josie recognised from her homeroom. Alex Hayes. The coach tossed her a basketball. "Let's see some shooting."

Josie's heart was thumping as she stood poised with the basketball in her hands and focused on the basket. It seemed so high, and so far away. She took a deep breath and threw.

The ball teetered on the rim of the basket and tumbled off. Josie ran forward and retrieved it, then cast a nervous look at the coach. "Do it again," he ordered.

Josie got back in position. Aiming carefully, she threw again. As the ball sailed through the air, she stared at it, willing it to go into the basket. It did! "Again," Coach Meadows bellowed.

Josie attempted ten throws, and six of them went through the basket. *Not bad*, she thought. She looked for a sign of approval on the coach's face, but it remained impassive.

"Let's see how you guard," he said. He and Alex joined her on the floor. Josie stood there with her knees slightly bent, her hands on her knees, and her eyes on the ball as she tried to anticipate the coach's moves. Then she bobbed back and forth in front of the boy, waving her arms as she tried to keep the ball from reaching him.

"Okay," the coach said. He tossed the ball to Alex. "Now, let me see you take it away from him." He went back to the sidelines.

With a friendly wink, Alex said, "I'm not going to make this easy for you." He started moving rapidly across the court while he dribbled the ball. He was pretty good, switching the ball's direction each time Josie got close. But she finally lunged in and snatched it away. Then she raced down the court, dribbling.

Coach Meadows blew his whistle and they stopped. Alex appraised Josie. "You're not bad."

"Thanks," Josie said. "Think I can get on the team?"

The boy grinned. "We'd put a monkey on the team if he could shoot a basket. Hey, Coach, you need me any more?"

The coach waved his hand in dismissal. "See ya," Alex said to Josie, and took off.

Josie approached the coach, who was writing something in a notebook. "How was I?"

He grunted. "You might work out. I have to talk to the boys." He peered at her keenly. "Having a girl on the team would be something new for them. Personally, I have no problem with that. But good basketball depends on teamwork and cooperation. The fellows might need some convincing."

Josie nodded.

The coach closed his notebook. "No promises. But I'll be in touch."

Josie didn't even bother to shower before changing back into her regular clothes. Okay, he'd said no promises, but he definitely sounded optimistic. And there was something about his gruffness that she found appealing. Mrs Parker, back at Willoughby Hall, had been like that sometimes. But deep inside she was soft and warm and caring. Maybe the coach was like that, too.

She ran all the way home, and she felt like she was flying.

For once, Josie was pleased that there weren't any customers in Morgan's Country Foods. Annie and Ben were behind the counter talking when she burst in.

"I tried out for the team," she told them. "And I think I might get on it!"

Ben slapped her gently on the back. "That's great!"

"Wonderful," Annie echoed, planting a kiss on Josie's forehead.

They did look pleased, but not quite as excited as Josie had expected them to be. "Is something wrong?" She asked.

Ben and Annie exchanged looks. "We were just talking about Cat and Becka," Ben said.

"What about them?" Josie asked.

Annie spoke hesitantly. "Josie . . . is there something going on between them? A disagreement?"

"Of course, you don't have to betray a confidence," Ben added quickly.

Josie shrugged. "I don't know. They might be having a little fight over something. Maybe it's got something to do with Becka hitting her with that pie on Saturday."

"But that was an accident, right?" Ben asked.

"Oh, sure," Josie said. "Look, don't worry about it. Whatever it is, it's no big deal."

"They just seem so tense with each other lately," Annie murmured. "They barely spoke to each other at dinner last night."

Ben snapped his fingers. "I'll bet I know what it's about. The bedroom."

Josie had completely forgotten about the soon-to-be-completed bedroom. "Yeah, maybe."

"Oh, dear," Annie sighed. "I was afraid it would cause friction. Maybe we should talk with them about it tonight. Have a real heart-to-heart talk."

"I'm not so sure that's the best approach," Ben said. "Did you read that article on sibling rivalry in the paper last Sunday? It said that adolescents should be given the opportunity to work out personal disagreements without parental involvement. Unless it goes on too long, of course."

"You're probably right," Annie said. "If we step in too soon, they might resent us."

Josie grinned. "Hey, they've been squabbling for thirteen years. I wouldn't worry about it if I were you."

"Oh, we're not worried," Ben said quickly.

"Of course not," Annie echoed. "And once you guys decide about the bedroom, everything will be fine. Right?"

"Sure," Josie said. But inside, she felt a little sorry for them. So far, ever since coming to the Morgans', the girls had been pretty much on their best behaviour – at least, in front of Annie and Ben. But were they really any closer than they'd been back at Willoughby Hall? Josie doubted it. And if Annie and Ben thought settling the matter of a bedroom would result in Cat and Becka being the best of friends . . . well, they still had a lot to learn about their daughters.

Six

"Oh, what a beautiful morning," Becka sang as she laid place mats on the dining room table. "Oh, what a beautiful day." That wasn't an accurate song in some ways. It wasn't morning. She was setting the table for dinner. And the day had been grey and cloudy, not particularly nice at all. None of that mattered. As far as Becka was concerned, everything was beautiful.

How her life had changed in just a few short days! One day she'd walked into school a pitiful nobody. Today, Tuesday, only one week and one day later, she was a real person. And she'd done it all on her own.

She caught a glimpse of herself in the mirror over the dining table, and her smile faded slightly. The beige shirtdress she wore made her skin look sallow. And it was so dull. But it was just like the kind of dress the girls in Heather's crowd wore. Heather herself had complimented Becka on it just that morning. Remembering that, she began to sing again.

Annie emerged from the kitchen with a stack of plates. "You sound happy."

"I am," Becka said.

Annie smiled. "I still can't get accustomed

to your new look. I liked your wild scarves and hats and all that. Of course, you still look lovely," she added quickly. "But what made you change your style so suddenly?"

"Oh, I don't know. Just felt like something new, I guess." Becka changed the subject. "You know, Annie, having friends makes all the difference in the world."

Annie put the plates down and swept her up in a quick hug. "I'm so glad! I could tell you were feeling lonely. Sometimes it's hard getting to know people when you're the new girl at school."

"No kidding," Becka said. "Especially for me. I guess I'm kind of shy."

Annie began distributing the plates. "That's why you're lucky to have sisters to help you out. I know Josie's been caught up in her basketball plans, but Cat –"

"I don't need Cat's help," Becka interrupted. "I've been making friends on my own."

Annie looked like she was about to say something, then caught herself. "Well, that's nice."

Josie came in from the kitchen. "The soup's simmering. It just needs a stir every few minutes. Can you guys handle that while I go wash up?"

"Stirring," Annie murmured. "Yes, I think we can manage. Josie, have you heard from the coach yet about the team?"

Josie shook her head. "I only tried out yesterday, though." She chewed on a fingernail. "I wonder if I could get Cat to put in a good word for me with Todd."

"I wouldn't count on that," Becka said. She recalled Cat's comments about Josie trying out for the team.

Annie looked at her in surprise. "Why not?"

Becka bit her lip. She didn't want to start any trouble. "Well, Cat's not very interested in sports."

"But she cares about what happens to Josie," Annie said.

"It's okay," Josie said quickly. "I don't need Cat's help. Hey, Becka, could you take a look at my book report tonight? See if I've made any major punctuation boo-boos?"

"Sure," Becka said.

As Josie ran out of the room, Annie looked after her thoughtfully, then turned to Becka. "Honey, I don't mean to pry, but you guys seem kind of down on Cat. Is there something going on I should know about?"

"Everything's fine," Becka assured her. When that didn't clear the concern on Annie's face, she added, "Maybe we're a little tense about this bedroom thing."

"Oh, dear. I don't want that to start a war between you."

"It won't," Becka said. "We'll work it out."

"Good. But you're sure nothing else is bothering you?"

Becka shook her head. At that very moment, nothing was bothering her. She felt so good about herself. Being in a group had given her so much confidence. Why, just today she'd smiled at two classmates she'd never looked at before – and they'd smiled back! Tomorrow, she might even talk to them.

Like Josie, she didn't need Cat, not for anything. And she barely looked up when Cat burst into the room. "Hi! I'm not late, am I?"

"Not this time," Annie said, smiling. "Where have you been?"

"Todd wanted me to watch his football practice." Cat made a face. "Talk about boring."

"When are we going to meet this Todd?" Annie asked.

"Maybe this weekend, when he asks me out for a real date."

"You sound pretty sure of yourself," Annie remarked.

Becka pretended to be concentrating on the correct placement of forks, spoons, and knives. But she was listening to every word.

Cat giggled. "If I want him to ask me out, he will. I might let him take me out after the pep rally on Friday. Just between us, I've got him wrapped around my little finger."

Annie raised her eyebrows. "I hope you're not taking advantage of that."

"I'm trying not to," Cat replied. "But it's not easy. He's such a pushover!" From upstairs came a pounding sound. "What's that?"

"Ben's working on the bedroom," Annie told her.

"I'm going to go see how it's coming along," Cat announced.

As soon as she left the room, Becka went to the phone in the kitchen. She dialled the number she already knew by heart.

"Heather, hey, it's me, Becka."

"Hi! Any news?"

Becka kept her voice low, so Annie, still in the dining room, couldn't hear her. "Cat went to Todd's football practice. And listen to what she said about him. She called him a pushover and says she's got him wrapped around her little finger."

She heard a sharp gasp at the other end. "Becka, you're terrific, a real friend. Hang on a second."

While she waited, Becka allowed herself a moment to bask in Heather's praise. Then her stomach started churning. It was a sensation that had become familiar recently, every time she played Mata Hari. She made a mental note to scratch international spying from her list of possible careers.

Heather returned. "Want to go to Brownies with me and Blair after school tomorrow?"

"Sure!"

She was just hanging up when Cat came in. "Talking to your best friend Heather?" she asked with a sneer.

Becka attempted an equally snide tone. "Why don't you just come right out and say it, Cat. You're jealous."

Cat's eyebrows practically met her hairline. "Jealous? Of *you*?"

"Because I'm friends with Heather Beaumont, who just happens to be one of the most important girls at school."

Cat uttered a short laugh. "Just because you've started to dress like her isn't going to make you two buddies. Although I have to say, it's an improvement on your old look. But you think she's your friend? Hah. No way."

"Oh yeah? Then why did she just invite me to go to Brownies with her after school tomorrow?" Becka challenged her.

Cat shrugged. "You got me. But I'll bet you anything she's got something up her sleeve. Face it, Becka. You're not in Heather Beaumont's league."

The churning in Becka's stomach ceased. Now she was boiling inside. But before she could strike back, Annie walked in.

The girls fell silent, but their expressions must have been dead giveaways. "What's going on?" Annie asked.

Cat immediately slipped on her sweetness-and-light mask. "We were just talking."

Annie's eyes moved back and forth between them. Then she sighed. "It's the bedroom, isn't it? You're arguing over who gets it."

"No, we're not," Becka said honestly.

"I'm just worried about Becka," Cat told Annie. "She's been hanging around with a girl who I don't think is very nice."

86

"That's crazy!" Becka exclaimed. "You're not worried. You don't think about anyone but yourself."

"Becka, that's not true," Annie said. "Cat's just showing sisterly concern."

Cat preened. "Of course I am."

"But I'm sure Becka is capable of choosing her own friends," Annie added. "You're both very different people, and it's not surprising that you have different friends."

Now it was Becka's turn to look smug. "Exactly."

Ben walked in. "Is this a private, all-girl discussion, or can anyone join in?"

"We were just clearing up a difference of opinion," Annie told him. "But everything's fine now. Right, girls?"

"That's right," Cat said.

"Absolutely," Becka echoed.

But as soon as their parents turned their backs, they exchanged stone-cold looks.

The next day, after the last bell, Cat stood by Todd's locker and tapped her foot impatiently. Where *was* he? He'd told her at lunch there was no football practice that day, and they could go to Brownies after school. Actually, he'd suggested Luigi's, for pizza, but she'd talked him into Brownies instead. She remembered Becka saying she'd be there with Heather. Cat was in the mood to do a little flaunting.

She looked up at the clock in the hall. He was ten minutes late. This was annoying.

Josie was coming down the hall. Cat noticed she wasn't walking in her usual brisk stride. She seemed to be dragging her feet.

"Hey, Josie," she called.

Josie paused. "Yeah?"

"Tell Annie I went to Brownies with Todd, okay?"

"Sure." Josie paused. "Listen, Cat . . ."

"What?"

This isn't going to be easy, Josie thought. She hated asking favours from Cat as much as Cat hated granting them. But she was desperate. "It's been two days since I tried out for the team, and I still haven't heard from Coach Meadows. I just went by his office, but he wasn't there."

"Oh, too bad." Cat peered down the rapidly emptying hallway. Todd was nowhere to be seen. Now she was really getting angry. He'd get two more minutes and that was it.

"So I was wondering . . ."

"What?" Cat asked testily.

"Maybe you could say something to Todd. I mean, he *is* the captain, so maybe he's heard something. . . ."

"I'm not asking him any favours for you," Cat said sharply. "Personally, I think your whole idea's nuts. Besides, the way I'm feeling about Todd right now –"

"Forget it," Josie snapped. "I should have

known better than to expect any help from you." She turned and walked away.

Cat couldn't help feeling a brief flicker of remorse. She probably shouldn't have spoken to Josie like that. But her annoyance was growing. Finally, Cat saw Todd approaching.

She better let him know right away she wasn't pleased about being kept waiting, she decided. So she just kept her mouth in a tight line as he approached.

Then she realised he wasn't smiling, either. And before she could say, "It's about time," he spoke.

"So you think I'm a pushover, huh?"

Cat's mouth fell open. She tried to say something, but all that came out was, "What?"

"You think you've got me wrapped around your little finger? Well, forget it. And forget about Luigi's, or Brownies, or wherever we were supposed to go." And with that, he turned his back on her and strode down the hall.

Cat was in a state of shock. It took several minutes for his words to penetrate. Then, fury rose up inside her.

Becka. It had to be her. Just wait till Cat got her hands on her.

Brownies was packed with the after-school crowd. Becka saw several kids from her classes, and it pleased her to know she was being seen with Heather and Blair.

She wished she could like Blair better,

though. There was something about her that made Becka feel uneasy, like Blair was evaluating her for a grade or something. And so far, she wasn't giving Becka an A plus.

"What's that thing around your neck?" Blair asked.

Becka fingered the scarf. "It's called a feather boa. They were very popular in the 1920s."

"Then what are you wearing it now for?"

"I like wearing unusual clothes," Becka said. "They're like costumes. They make me feel as if I'm a character in a book."

Blair's upper lip curled. "Why don't you save them for Hallowe'en?"

Becka stared down at the table. She'd thought, now that she was in the "in" crowd, she could afford to add a little sparkle to these dreary clothes. Obviously, that was a mistake.

But Heather's next words cheered her immensely. "Now, Blair," Heather said. "Becka's got a perfect right to dress the way she likes. I think she looks very interesting."

That shut Blair up.

"I saw Todd today," Heather continued. "He asked me to go out with him after the pep rally on Friday."

"What did you tell him?" Blair asked.

"I said maybe. *If* he did me a little favour first."

"What kind of favour?" Becka asked.

"Oh, just some little thing," Heather said vaguely.

"Wow, Cat's going to be surprised," Becka noted. "I think she was expecting him to ask her out this weekend."

Heather laughed lightly. "I don't think she'll be so surprised. Now that he knows what she's been saying about him, I don't think she'll be expecting a call."

Becka almost choked on her ice cream. "You told him what I told you?" *Why didn't I see that coming?* Becka thought angrily. *I'm such a dope!*

"Of course," Heather said. "Why do you think I wanted you to spy on her for me?" She leaned forward, and her green eyes bored into Becka's. "Don't be mad. You know Cat would have done the same thing. I'm just lucky I have you on my side."

Becka managed a thin smile. Heather was probably right. But she was thinking about the scene at home tonight.

"And like you said," Heather continued, "you're not really sisters. You don't owe her anything."

Becka thought back to the first week of school. She thought back to Willoughby Hall, all the nasty things Cat had done to her and said to her over the years, picking on her, poking fun at her, calling her a wimp. Heather was right. Cat wasn't a sister. She wasn't even a friend.

"Speaking of the pep rally," Blair murmured, and she shot a meaningful look at Heather.

"Oh, right." Heather smiled brightly at Becka. "I've got a big surprise for you."

"A surprise?"

"But you have to keep it a secret," Heather cautioned. "Before I tell you, promise me you won't tell anyone."

"I promise," Becka said.

"Well, this is the first pep rally of the year. As captain of the cheerleaders, I want to do something different. Instead of leading the first cheer, I've decided to invite a student to lead it. And the student I've picked" – she paused dramatically – "is you!"

"Me?" Becka squeaked.

Heather nodded. Then she leaned back in her seat and smiled.

Becka was nonplussed. "But – but what do I do? I don't know anything about cheerleading."

"You don't need to," Heather said. "All you do is stand in front of the cheerleading squad and yell, 'Are you ready?' That's how we always start the first cheer. The crowd will yell, 'Yeah,' or something like that. Then the cheerleaders start the cheer, and you just clap your hands in rhythm."

"In front of the whole school?" Becka asked faintly.

"Of course! Becka, do you realise what a big honour this is? We're starting a new tradition! And after this, *everyone* will know who you are."

Becka pictured herself, standing in front of the bleachers, the eyes of every student on her.

"Oh, Heather! You really want *me* to do that?"

"Absolutely. You're my number-one choice."

Chills ran through Becka. She'd be famous! When Cat heard about this, she would be positively green with envy!

As if reading her mind, Heather repeated her earlier warning. "Remember what I said. This is a secret. No one can know until you actually come out on the gym floor."

Again, Becka promised she wouldn't tell. She knew that wasn't going to be easy. Next to being adopted, this had to be the most exciting thing that had ever happened to her. All the way home, she envisioned herself at the pep rally, surrounded by congratulating admirers.

She'd almost forgotten about Cat and Todd. But when she walked into their bedroom, Cat's face reminded her. And if Cat's angry expression wasn't enough, the furious words that followed did the trick.

"You *sneak*!" Cat yelled. "How could you do that to me?"

Becka considered pretending she didn't know what Cat was talking about. But what was the point?

"You didn't really care about Todd," Becka retorted. "You were just using him to get back at Heather."

"And Heather's just using you to get back at me," Cat shot back. "I can't believe you're so dumb you can't figure that out."

"Heather's my friend," Becka replied. "Which is more than you've ever been."

"Right, she's your friend." Sarcasm dripped from Cat's words. "You just wait. Now that she's got Todd, she'll dump you. You'll see."

"That's not true!"

"Oh yeah?"

"Yeah! As a matter of fact –" Becka stopped. But she couldn't resist a little hint. "For your information, she chose me for a big honour. It's something very exciting and very important. Something that's going to make me famous."

"Yeah, in your dreams," Cat snorted. "What kind of honour?"

"I – I can't tell you. It's a secret. Just wait till the pep rally on Friday," Becka began, then caught herself.

"What's going to happen at the pep rally?"

"You'll see," Becka said mysteriously. Just let Cat try to pry this out of her!

She was mildly disappointed when all she got was a scathing look. "You're just having another one of your fantasies."

"I am not! You think *you're* hot stuff! Wait till after the pep rally!"

Becka must have gotten through to her. It was a pleasure to see Cat actually looking uncertain. It was even better to watch her storm out of the room.

Marla's voice on the other end of the line

was incredulous. "What kind of honour could Heather give Becka?"

"I have no idea," Cat said. "All I know is that it's got something to do with the pep rally on Friday. I don't think she was making it up. What do you think this is all about?"

"I don't know," Marla said, sounding troubled. "Something's up. Heather's got some sort of scheme. I *told* you she wasn't through getting even with you."

"But what could she do to Becka at a pep rally?"

"Maybe I could find out what's going on," Marla said. "I'll ask around."

"Don't bother," Cat replied. "After what Becka did to me? Telling Heather what I said about Todd? She deserves *anything* Heather's got planned for her."

"She's still your sister," Marla reminded her.

Some sister, Cat thought as she said goodbye and hung up. *Traitor's more like it*. Heather was nuts if she thought something nasty happening to Becka would bother Cat. If something awful did happen to Becka at the pep rally, it served her right. Cat was actually curious to see what Heather had in store for her.

Seven

Somehow, Becka managed to keep her secret to herself the next day at school. It wasn't easy. Every time she heard someone mention the pep rally, it was all she could do to keep from shouting, "And I'm going to lead the first cheer!"

In her last class of the day, American history, there was a pop quiz. Becka finished in twenty minutes, took a few more minutes to check her answers, and then settled back for some serious daydreaming.

The images that formed in her head were wonderful. She saw the entire student body watching her perform the first cheer and asking each other, "Why haven't we noticed that cute girl before?" She saw herself besieged with invitations to go out after the rally.

She was so lucky to have a friend like Heather. What had she done to deserve this good fortune? Of all the kids at school, why had Heather bestowed this honour on her?

Because Heather liked her, of course. Still, in the back of her mind, there was a niggling suspicion that maybe it was something she'd earned, a reward for services rendered. Maybe it was Heather's way of saying thanks for spying on Cat and passing on the information.

Well, even if it was, so what? Now that Heather had Todd back, Becka wouldn't have to spy anymore. She and Heather could be normal friends. She didn't have to feel guilty about Cat. After all, Cat would have done something like that to her. Something worse, even.

When Becka left class, she went directly to the library, where she'd promised to meet Louise. She found her at a corner table poring over her book report, which was due the next day. "Could you read it over for me?" she asked Becka. "By the way, I actually liked that book about the doctor. It was really interesting."

You'd never know it by reading the report, Becka thought. It was dull and dry, just the facts of the story and not much else. But that was Louise's style, and there wasn't much Becka could do about it.

"It's okay," she said.

"But boring, right?" Louise asked. That fact didn't seem to bother her. "That's what my brother said."

"Louise . . . do you and your brother get along?"

"Are you kidding?" Louise made a face. "He's a pain. And he always gets his way. For example, I wanted to set up a chemistry lab in our basement. He wanted to turn it into a games room. Guess what we got?"

"Cat's like that," Becka said. "She always gets her way."

"And he's always teasing me," Louise continued. "Calling me Doctor Frankenstein and stuff like that."

So brothers aren't any better than sisters, Becka thought.

"It's funny, though," Louise said. "He's always putting me down. But when a friend of his started teasing me once, my brother told him to cut it out. I guess I'm the same way about him. I mean, *I* can criticise him. But I wouldn't let someone else."

Becka thought about this. So there *was* a difference. It made her feel uncomfortable. Would she ever feel that way about Josie and Cat? Would they ever feel that way about her? Suddenly, she wanted to change the subject. "You going to the pep rally tomorrow night?"

"I haven't decided. I don't usually go to things like that. I hate crowds. But I might go to this one – something funny is going to happen."

"Oh yeah? How do you know?"

"Someone called my brother to hire a clown."

"What's the clown going to do?" Becka asked.

"He's supposed to ride a bicycle across the gym and hit the person leading the first cheer in the face with a pie. Won't that be a scream? A cheerleader with cream pie all over her face?"

Becka sat very still.

"Becka? Don't you think it's funny?"

Could someone actually feel hot and cold

98

and numb, all at the same time? With some difficulty, Becka asked the next question. "Who – who ordered the clown?"

"Heather Beaumont." Louise frowned. "Wait, that's weird. *She'd* be leading the cheers, right? I can't picture her wanting to get hit with a pie, can you?"

"No."

Louise eyed her quizzically. "Hey, aren't you friends with her? I wonder why she didn't tell you about this. I guess maybe she wants it to be a big surprise."

"Yes," Becka said. "It's a big surprise." She rose. "I have to go." Somehow, with a great deal of effort, she managed to get one foot in front of the other until she was out of the library.

Josie rapped on Coach Meadows's door. This time, the coach actually looked up. "Come in, Josie. Have a seat."

His expression wasn't anywhere near as fierce as she remembered, and he was certainly being a lot friendlier. That was a good sign. "I got a message you wanted to see me," Josie said. She sat down on the chair by his desk.

The coach nodded. Then he started rapping a pencil on his desk. Josie waited. Finally, he spoke.

"Josie, you're a pretty decent basketball player. I have a feeling you'd be an asset to the team."

"Thanks, Coach," Josie began, but he held up his hand.

"There's a problem. It seems the team doesn't have quite the same feelings."

"They don't?" Josie asked faintly.

Coach Meadows scowled. "To tell you the truth, I don't understand it. They're solid boys, and I always figured them to be pretty open-minded. But I guess I overestimated them. According to the captain, the boys wouldn't be comfortable with a girl on the team."

As the meaning of his words sunk in, Josie had a sinking sensation. "Why not? It's not like we'd be sharing a locker room!"

The coach threw up his hands. "It makes no sense to me, either. But like I told you before, Josie, a team's got to be able to work together. We can't afford any hostilities. I can't force you on them. They'll resent me, and you, and that kind of attitude doesn't make for a winning team."

"I understand," Josie said dully. She stood up. "I wouldn't want to be on a team that didn't want me anyway."

"I'm sorry, Josie," Coach Meadows said, and he sounded like he really was. "But unless the boys change their minds . . ."

Josie nodded and went to the door. With her hand on the knob, she turned back. "You said the captain told you this?"

"Yeah. Speaking for the team."

"That's Todd Murphy, right?"

The coach nodded.

"Well, thanks anyway." Josie left and walked down the hall towards the exit. Fury burned inside her, and she knew where to direct it. Not at the coach. Not even at Todd Murphy. The object of her anger was closer to home.

She'd accepted the fact that Cat wouldn't help her get on the team. But she hadn't expected Cat to go out of her way to *hurt* her chances.

Cat sat on the gym bleachers next to Marla and half listened as the pep club secretary finished his report.

". . . so the total from the bake sale comes to one hundred and fifty dollars. That's not enough for new basketball uniforms, so we need ideas for more fundraising." He stepped aside, and Heather stood before the group.

"I want to remind everyone about the pep rally tomorrow afternoon. As you know, it's the first rally of the season. All the football players and cheerleaders will be introduced, and we have to show them that we support them."

"I'd like to support her right out of town," Marla whispered to Cat.

Cat managed a small smile. Thinking about football players made her think about Todd. She couldn't exactly say her heart was broken, but knowing he was back with Heather was just so aggravating.

"It's going to be a great rally," Heather continued, "and there just may be some surprises!"

Marla clutched Cat's arm and whispered, "Maybe she's going to say something about Becka."

Cat shrugged. Even so, she cleared her head and concentrated on what Heather was saying. But Heather just went on to give a standard pep talk on school spirit. Then the meeting was over.

Cat, Marla, and Britt left the building together. "I asked around," Marla said, "but nobody could tell me anything. I still don't know what Heather's got up her sleeve."

"Maybe it's nothing," Cat said. "I mean, she's got Todd back. Wouldn't she be satisfied with that?"

"Heather's never satisfied," Marla noted. She turned to Britt. "Remember, back in fifth grade, when she got mad at you for wearing the same dress she was wearing to a birthday party?"

Britt twisted a strand of her golden brown hair. "I certainly do. And I remember when she accidentally on purpose spilled a glass of grape Kool-Aid all over mine."

"That wasn't the end of it, either," Marla told Cat. "For the next month, she made Britt's life miserable."

"What did she do?" Cat asked in horrified fascination.

"Lots of things," Britt said. "Like, she was always watching me in class, so if I passed a note or something, she'd tell the teacher."

"See?" Marla said to Cat. "Heather never gives up when she wants revenge."

"She stops at nothing," Britt added.

Cat tried not to let their ominous tone get to her. But by now she knew these girls well enough to know they wouldn't exaggerate. They were her friends, and their concern for her was sincere.

Still, she wasn't completely convinced that Becka was in danger. "Who knows? Maybe Heather really likes Becka."

Britt shook her head. "Come on, Cat, you said yourself Becka's not her type. You told us she's a wimp and a daydreamer and completely out of it."

"She's not *that* awful," Cat began, but then she stopped. What was she defending *her* for?

Marla looked thoughtful. "We could be wrong, I guess. I mean, maybe she's planning something for the other one. What's her name?"

"Josie," Cat murmured. "Nah, she couldn't hurt Josie. Josie's tough and down-to-earth. She knows how to take care of herself." She noticed that both Britt and Marla were looking at her with mild surprise on their faces. "What?"

"That's the first time you've ever mentioned her without putting her down," Marla said.

"Yeah?" Cat thought about that. "I guess you're right. Of course, there's a lot to put down about her. She's immature, she doesn't know how to dress, her hair's a disaster, and she acts more like a boy than a girl."

103

"Yeah, you three sure don't seem like sisters," Marla remarked.

"You don't act like sisters either," Britt added. "You guys really don't have anything to do with each other, do you?"

"Well, we've got absolutely nothing in common," Cat said. "Except parents."

Marla laughed. "That's what I'm always telling *my* sister."

"Oh, your sister's not so awful," Britt said. "A little bossy, maybe, and selfish, but she's not horrible."

"Mmm, maybe. She can be a creep sometimes, but I have to admit, I can count on her."

"For what?" Cat asked.

"I don't know. Just . . . to be there for me, I guess. To be on my side. You know what I mean."

Cat wasn't sure.

The girls separated to go on to their own homes. Walking into the old farmhouse, Cat heard the sound of a drill upstairs. She went up there and found Ben at the end of the hall working in the bedroom-to-be.

"Where is everyone?" Cat asked.

Ben turned off the drill. "Annie's at the store. I don't know where Becka and Josie are. How was your day?"

"Fine." Cat wandered around the bare room. The wood floor had been stripped and polished and it glowed. It was a nice-sized room, small enough to be cosy but big enough for everything a person needed in a bedroom. Sunshine streamed in from the two big windows that overlooked the flower garden. "This is going to be a beautiful room."

"Thanks," Ben said. "I'll be able to start painting in a few days."

Cat studied the walls. "I'd like pale yellow. Or maybe a very light green. And striped curtains. No, wait. Maybe those modern blinds, the really thin ones, in the same colour as the walls. Or a shade darker." Looking around the room, she could almost see it the way she wanted it to be.

"It sounds like a decision's been made," Ben said. Cat's vision dissolved.

"Well, no," she admitted. She flashed Ben a dazzling smile. "I just keep thinking of it as mine."

Ben smiled back, but his face was serious. "I think you'd better take the fact that you have two sisters into consideration before you start decorating."

Reluctantly, Cat nodded. "Yeah. I know."

"I'm going to work on this floor a little more," Ben said. He pointed to a box of tools and rags in the corner. "Cat, could you get that out of the way for me? Take it out to the barn?"

"Sure," Cat said. Being a good daughter was getting easier all the time. She picked up the box and carried it downstairs.

She went across the grassy yard to the barn.

Since her arms were occupied with the box, she pushed the barn door open with her hip.

Squinting into the dim light, she froze when she heard a sound coming from a back corner. It was probably just a chicken that had got out of the coop, she thought. Then she listened closer. No, it wasn't a chicken.

Cat put the box down and followed the sound of muffled sobs. Behind the lawn mower, a small figure lay huddled on the floor.

Cat had seen Becka cry before. For thirteen years, Cat had been a witness to her whimpers and sniffles again and again. Becka cried more easily than anyone Cat had ever known. But not like this.

Cat edged around her, stepping over bags of chicken feed. Becka acknowledged her presence by lifting her pale, tear-streaked face.

"Why are you crying?" Cat asked.

She could just barely make out Becka's response. "You wouldn't understand." Becka buried her face in her hands again.

Cat stood there uneasily. That wasn't like Becka. Usually, she was more than willing to tell anyone who'd listen why she was upset.

"Did something bad happen?"

Becka didn't answer and she still had her face covered. Her whole body was shaking.

Cat could have just walked out and left Becka to pull herself together. But for some reason, she didn't.

"What happened?" she asked again.

Slowly, Becka came out of her curled-up position and sat up. "What do you care?"

"Just curious," Cat said. Becka's face was all wet and grimy from lying on the floor. It wasn't very pleasant looking. Cat pulled off the little scarf tied around her own neck. "Here. Wipe your face."

Becka obliged. Eyeing the floor with distaste, Cat got an old worn-out quilt and put it down before joining Becka.

"What's the big problem? Got an A minus on a test?"

Becka's head moved from side to side. Cat sighed and tried to be patient. Finally, in a halting voice, Becka spoke.

"Remember what I told you about the pep rally? About Heather giving me a big honour?"

Cat had a sinking feeling she was about to hear something pretty bad. "Yeah. You going to finally tell me what it is?"

Becka's voice quavered. "She wanted me to lead the first cheer at the pep rally. Take her place as head cheerleader."

"You're kidding!" Cat exclaimed. "That doesn't sound like Heather, giving up the spotlight."

"You're right. It was all a trick. She hired a clown to come to the rally and hit me in the face with a pie. Right in front of the whole school." Becka burst into tears again.

Cat could hear her own sharp intake of breath. Slowly, she let it out. "Wow." It was a vast understatement, considering the circumstances.

"I thought she was my friend," Becka wailed.

"She's nobody's friend," Cat stated. "I told you she couldn't be trusted."

"But she was nice to me," Becka protested, weeping. "She talked to me. Hardly anyone else did that. Not even you."

Cat winced. She couldn't exactly deny it.

"Why would she do this to *me*?" Becka asked brokenly.

"She wants to get back at me," Cat said. "For flirting with Todd." As an afterthought, she added, "And for being prettier than she is."

Becka looked confused. "I don't get it. How does hurting me get back at you?"

"Well, we're both Morgans. She figured I'd feel bad if people were laughing at you."

"That still doesn't make sense," Becka said, wiping her nose. "You wouldn't care if I was embarrassed in front of the whole school."

Cat's next words slipped out before she even thought of them. "Yes, I would."

That obviously came as a shock to Becka, and Cat couldn't blame her. It was a shock to *her*, too.

"You would? Why?"

"I don't know why," Cat said. She tried to sound nonchalant. "I guess because, well, like I said before, we're in the same family."

"You mean . . . because we're sisters now."

Becka's sad, wistful expression was painful to face. Cat looked away. "Yeah." She glanced back with apprehension. She hoped Becka wouldn't use this as an excuse to get all sloppy and mushy and hug her or something.

She didn't. But her look of astonishment was almost as hard to bear. Then Cat found herself doing something totally out of character. She reached out and awkwardly patted Becka's shoulder.

That brought forth another flood of tears.

"It's okay," Cat murmured. "At least now you know the truth about her. Just think, if you hadn't found out in time . . ." The thought of Becka standing in front of the laughing crowd made Cat shudder.

After a moment, Becka's tears subsided. "I guess I just won't go."

"Oh, yes you will," Cat retorted briskly.

"I will?"

"You're not going to give her the satisfaction of knowing she scared you away. I wish I could get my hands on Heather Beaumont right this minute. Except that she's not worth going to jail for."

For a few minutes, the girls sat there silently. Cat was lost in thought, a zillion emotions churning inside her. There was anger at Heather, sympathy for Becka, and the violent desire to do something about this mess.

Before she could straighten out her feelings, the barn door flew open. Josie stood there.

"What are you doing here?" Cat asked.

"I was looking for a place to be alone." Josie

turned to leave, but she must have caught a glimpse of Becka's face. She came forward. "What did you do to *her*?"

Cat raised her eyebrows. "Nothing. For your information, Becka's just had a big shock. I'm trying to help her."

"Sure you are." Josie's eyes were flashing. "Just like you helped me."

"Helped you do what?" Cat asked.

Josie put her hands on her hips. "Just out of curiosity, Cat, what did you bribe him with? Your undying love and affection?"

Cat gazed at her in bewilderment. "What are you talking about?"

Josie's upper lip curled. "Don't you dare play little Miss Sweetsy-Cutesy with me. I just talked to Coach Meadows. You'll be very happy to know your rotten scheme worked."

"What did I do?" Cat asked.

Josie snorted. "You know what you did."

"Josie! Tell me what you think I did!"

"It's not what I think, it's what I know. You got a message to Coach Meadows that the boys didn't want me on the basketball team."

Cat gasped. *"What?"*

"You heard me."

"I didn't do that!"

"Oh, give me a break!" Josie exclaimed. "I'm not stupid, Cat. You might be able to pull off that innocent act with Annie and Ben, but I know you. You thought I'd look stupid playing basketball with boys, and I'd embarrass you. So

110

you made sure I wouldn't get on the team."

Becka's soft, trembling voice broke in. "Cat, how could you do that to Josie?"

Cat leaped to her feet. "I'm telling you, I didn't do anything!"

For a second, a glimmer of doubt crossed Josie's face. Then it disappeared. "The facts speak for themselves."

"Tell me exactly what the coach told you," Cat demanded.

"Like you don't know."

"Tell me!" Cat insisted.

Josie groaned. "All right, if it'll make you happy. Todd Murphy told the coach the boys don't want me on the team."

"Todd!" Cat put a hand to her head. Was she losing her mind? "That's weird. He told me he wouldn't care if a girl was on the team."

"Of course he wouldn't mind!" Josie said. "None of the boys I talked to cared. But *you* didn't want me on the team. So you got Todd to lie and tell Coach Meadows not to put me on the team."

"No, I didn't! I've hardly even talked to Todd in two days!"

"Oh yeah? Then why would he say something like that to the coach?"

It didn't take long for Cat to figure it out. She sank back down to the floor. "Marla was right," she whispered.

"What does Marla have to do with this?" Becka asked.

111

"She said Heather Beaumont would try to get back at me through you guys."

Now it was Josie's turn to look confused. "What does Heather Beaumont have to do with this?"

"Don't you see?" Cat asked. "Heather told Todd to keep you off the team."

Josie got down on the floor, too. "Why would she do that? I don't even know Heather Beaumont."

"But she knows who you are," Cat said. "At least, she knows you're my sister. Boy, Marla wasn't kidding. When Heather wants revenge, she goes all out." She told Josie what had happened to Becka.

When she finished the story, Josie was stunned. "That girl is *evil*."

"That's putting it mildly," Cat muttered.

Becka actually looked frightened. "Is she going to be picking on us from now on?"

"Jeez," Josie murmured. "I've never had anyone do something like this to me before."

"It's my fault," Cat said. "I'm the one she's really out to get. She's *my* enemy."

"It looks like she's *our* enemy now," Josie noted.

"Yeah," Becka said. "She's out to get all of us."

Sadly, Cat nodded. There was a silence as they all three contemplated this.

Then Cat raised her head. "But we don't have to sit still and take it."

"What choice do we have?" Josie asked.

Cat got up and began to pace. "We've got a choice. I'll tell you this: as far as I'm concerned, the Morgan sisters aren't about to let this . . . this *witch* stomp all over us. Hey, remember when we told Annie and Ben we were a team?"

Josie uttered a short laugh. "The whopper of the century."

"Okay, maybe it was," Cat said. "But we need to be a team now, if we're going to survive Green Falls Junior High. *And* Heather Beaumont."

"She's right," Becka said to Josie. "We're all in this together."

"And we're not going to let her get away with this," Cat stated firmly.

"What are we going to do?" Josie asked.

"I'm not sure yet," Cat said, still pacing. "But I'll think of something. We're not going to sit around and cry, or just get mad." She whirled around and faced them.

"We're going to get even."

Eight

Why did Josie always have to make French toast on mornings Becka couldn't eat? Poking at her food, Becka's thoughts kept turning to the plans they'd made for the day. She went over and over them, hoping she'd get them right.

Josie was eating with fierce determination. She cut her food, speared it, and chewed it in a steady rhythm. Becka knew from experience that meant *she* was deep in thought, too.

Only Cat seemed to be able to pretend this was an ordinary day. She prattled on in her usual fashion while she ate.

"I like my French class," she was telling Annie and Ben. "Mademoiselle Casalls is so neat. She's got the cutest accent. And she's very chic. She goes to France every summer and buys all her clothes in Paris."

Ben smiled. "I guess that's what makes a good teacher, right?"

"Absolutely," Cat said. "Personally, I think it's much easier to learn from someone who looks good."

"By the way," Annie said to Ben, "I saw in the paper this morning there's a sale on paint at the hardware store. Do you want to pick some up this afternoon?"

"I could," Ben said, "but I don't know what colour to get. Girls, have you made a decision?"

"About what?" Becka asked.

"The new bedroom."

The girls exchanged looks. Cat spoke for them. "We really haven't talked about it yet."

"But I thought that's what you were doing last night," Annie said. "You guys were being so secretive, holed up in your room and talking till all hours."

"And you two have been very quiet this morning," Ben added, with a nod toward Becka and Josie.

Becka smiled nervously. Thank goodness Cat had the cool to handle comments like this. "I guess we're all thinking about the pep rally after school today. We're pretty excited."

That's putting it mildly, Becka thought.

"We were talking about maybe bringing some friends back here afterwards," Cat went on.

Becka looked at her in surprise. "We were?"

Cat ignored that. "Would that be okay?" she asked Annie and Ben.

"Sure," Annie said. "It sounds like fun. We could have a cookout."

Becka hoped Cat's response would satisfy Annie and Ben's curiosity. But after breakfast, when she ran back up to their room to get her books, Annie stopped her in the hall. "Becka, is everything okay?"

115

Becka attempted an imitation of Cat's casual smoothness. "Yeah, everything's fine."

Annie looked sceptical. "Is there anything you want to talk about?"

"No . . ."

Annie's penetrating gaze caused Becka to drop her eyes. but when she raised them, she saw that Annie was smiling.

"I guess some things have to be just between sisters."

Becka smiled back. "Yeah." She ran downstairs to join the others.

The girls didn't get a chance to confer again until Ben dropped them off at school. As they walked to the entrance, Cat went over the plans. "Don't forget what you have to find out," she warned Becka. "And don't be obvious! You have to act like everything's normal and you don't know anything."

Becka shivered. "I hope I can pull it off."

"You *have* to," Cat said sternly. She turned to Josie. "And *you*, don't say anything to anyone about anything. If Becka plays her part right, I'll be in a position to help you."

Josie eyed her suspiciously. "I'm still not so sure I can trust you."

"Trust me," Cat stated. "Like I said, we're in this together. And if everything goes according to plan, we're all going to benefit." She gave final instructions to Becka. "Leave lunch early and meet me at twelve-thirty in the library."

The girls separated and Becka went on to her

homeroom. When she got there, she waved to Louise in the back and took her own seat up front. Right after Mr Gorgeous Davison took roll, a student came into the room with a note for him.

Mr Davison read it and spoke to the class. "I have to go to the office for a minute. Don't throw any wild parties while I'm gone."

The minute he was out the door, people started talking and moving about. "He's so cute," Becka thought, and then she flushed when she realised she'd spoken out loud.

The short, fair-haired girl sitting next to her turned. "Tell me about it." She cocked her head towards the girl on her other side. "Lisa almost passes out when he walks in every day."

Lisa grinned, pushing her straight brown bangs out of her blue eyes. "I wouldn't talk if I were you." She leaned over towards Becka. "Patty turns beet red every time he calls her name in roll."

"Don't . . . don't you think he looks a little like that movie star in the *Superman* movies?" Becka asked.

"Exactly!" Patty said. "That's just what we were saying last week, right?"

Lisa nodded. She put a hand over her heart and pretended to swoon. "I'll bet he's a good kisser."

"We'll never find out," Patty sighed.

"I wonder if he's married," Becka mused.

"Why?" Lisa asked. "Think you've got a chance with him?"

They all started giggling. "I'm always looking for an excuse to talk to him," Patty told Becka. "Like, when he gets back, I'm going to ask him for a pass to the library." She pulled a fat book out of her purse. "Actually, I really do have to return this. I checked it out last June!"

Lisa whistled. "You're going to owe a fortune in fines."

"It won't be that bad," Patty said. "Ms Lesser doesn't charge for the summer. Anyway, she'll just be happy that I read the whole thing."

"What is it?" Becka asked.

"Gone With the Wind."

"I never read that. I saw the movie, though."

"The book's even better," Patty told her. She handed it to Becka, who opened it and scanned the first page.

Something caught her eye right away – a description of Scarlett O'Hara, with her black hair and green eyes. "She sounds like Cat," Becka thought. Once again, she had spoken aloud without meaning to.

"Cat Morgan?" Lisa asked. She turned to Patty. "She's in our biology class."

"Oh, yeah." Patty took the book back from Becka and looked at the page. "Hey, you're right. This description does match her."

"Not to mention the fact that she's a major flirt, too," Lisa added, looking over Patty's shoulder.

"But she's really okay," Becka said.

"Your name's Morgan, too, right?" Lisa asked. "Are you guys related?"

"Sort of," Becka said. "Well, more than sort of. We're sisters."

"Gee, you two don't look a bit alike," Patty commented.

Becka fingered a lock of her blonde hair. "We're adopted."

"You're kidding!" Lisa exclaimed. "I'm adopted, too!" She looked at Becka with interest. "Do you ever wonder about your birth parents?"

"Sometimes," Becka admitted.

At that moment, Mr Davison returned and they had to stop talking. But when the bell rang, Lisa immediately turned to Becka. "You want to sit with us at lunch today?"

Becka was about to say yes when she remembered. She shook her head with real regret. "I can't today. But how about Monday?"

As she walked with them out of the room, she wondered why she'd never tried talking to them before. They were so nice! And they had so much in common. It was funny how talking with them felt different than when she talked with Heather and Blair. She hadn't thought about how she looked, and she hadn't felt the need to consider everything she said before she said it. They'd both been so friendly. It gave Becka a warm feeling that lasted all morning. And the boost of confidence she was going to need to get through lunch.

In the cafeteria, Becka picked up her lunch tray without even noticing what it contained. She knew she wouldn't be able to eat. In the back of her mind, she was thinking that it was too bad she couldn't stay this nervous all the time. She'd certainly never have to worry again about gaining weight.

Heather, Blair, and Eve were already seated at their table. Becka stretched her lips into something she hoped would pass for a smile. She recalled the time when she thought she might want to be an actress someday. Here was her chance to find out if she had any talent at all.

She was amazed at the way Heather greeted her with such a bright, warm, cheery smile. Talk about acting ability.

"Hi, Becka! Excited about this afternoon?"

Blair made a funny sound, something between a giggle and a cough. Eve stared down at her lunch.

"Oh, I am!" Becka exclaimed. "I can't wait!"

"I'll bet Cat's really jealous," Blair said.

Remembering Cat's instructions, Becka nodded eagerly. "Oh, definitely. You know how she likes to be the centre of attention all the time."

Heather beamed. "Well, today *you'll* be the centre of attention. Everyone will be talking about you for days to come."

Blair started doing that weird giggle-cough again, but she stopped suddenly and winced. Becka figured Heather must have kicked her under the table.

"Even Josie's jealous," Becka continued. "Of course, she's pretty down anyway. She didn't get on the basketball team."

Eve's head jerked up. "She didn't?"

"No, the team captain told the coach they didn't want any girls playing with them."

Eve looked stunned. "Todd did that?" She turned to Heather in dismay. "Oh, Heather, you didn't . . ." Her voice trailed off as Heather fixed ice-cold eyes on her. Becka almost felt sorry for her. Heather obviously had Eve under her thumb.

Becka glanced at the clock. She only had ten minutes before she had to meet Cat, and she still needed to get some information. "Are you going out with Todd after the rally?" she asked in an offhand way.

"We're meeting at Brownies," Heather told her.

Becka became totally alert. "You're not leaving the rally together?"

"No, he's got a football team meeting. And I want to go home and change first."

"What time are you meeting him?"

"Five o'clock." Heather looked at Becka sharply. "How come you're so interested in me and Todd?"

Becka thought rapidly, then uttered a coy giggle. "Well, after all, I did help get you guys back together. I can't help being interested."

Heather studied her thoughtfully. "You know, I have to admit, Becka, I was a little surprised that you did that for me. I mean, I know you and Cat and Josie don't get along. But you *are* sisters. I'll bet deep down inside you guys care about what happens to each other. Like, I'm sure you and Cat feel bad about Josie right now." She waited for Becka's reaction.

Becka was boiling inside, and it was all she could do to keep from picking up her milk and throwing it in Heather's face. But she couldn't blow it now. Heather would get hers.

"Oh, you never know," Becka said lightly. "Tell me how it's going to be at the pep rally. Do you introduce me?"

She listened carefully to Heather's explanation. Then she looked at the clock again. "Okay. I'm sure I can do that. I've got to go now."

"It's not time for class yet," Eve pointed out.

"I know. But I have to return a book to the library. It's way overdue." How easy the lies were coming! Maybe she should consider an acting career after all.

She returned her untouched tray and hurried to the library. Cat was waiting. "Well, what did you find out?"

Becka reported on the conversation. Cat was particularly interested in the details of Heather's date with Todd after the rally. And Becka didn't feel bad about being Mata Hari this one last time. After all, she owed Heather nothing.

"They're not leaving the rally together.

Fantastic." Cat led Becka to a table in the corner and ripped two sheets of paper out of her notebook. "Now, where did she say they were planning to meet?"

"At Brownies."

Becka watched as Cat carefully pencilled a note. It read, "Todd, let's meet at Luigi's instead. Love, Heather."

"Won't he be able to tell that's not her handwriting?" Becka asked.

Cat shook her head. "I don't think Todd's the type who would remember what someone's handwriting looks like. Now for the next one." On the second paper, she wrote:

> *Even though I never speak to you at school, I've had a secret crush on you for ages. I'll be at Brownies at five o'clock today, and I hope you'll be there, too.*
>
> *Heather Beaumont*

"Whew," Becka said in awe. "Heather's going to be furious with you."

"That's the general idea," Cat reminded her. "And after this pep rally, she'll think twice before she messes with *you* too." She folded the paper and handed it to Becka. "Here, you know what to do with it." She folded the first note. "I'll take care of this one." Her eyes glittered like emeralds.

"Cat," Becka said, "are you still interested in Todd? Or are you just using him?"

"I don't know," Cat said thoughtfully. "Anyway, if I *am* using him, he deserves it. After what he did to Josie."

Becka looked at her in wonder. "Then, you're not doing all this just to get even. You really care about me and Josie."

Cat just shrugged. Becka had a feeling she could take that to mean yes. She was filled with a warm, cosy sensation. "We care about you, too."

Cat groaned. "Becka, don't get mushy. And you better hurry. It's almost time for class."

Becka left the library and went to the main hall, where most of the lockers were located. At this time of day, right after lunch, it was crowded with kids putting books into their lockers and taking them out. Becka wandered up and down the hall, keeping her eyes peeled for a likely candidate.

She spotted one. He was a greaser, one of the boys who'd been with the crowd she'd sat with at lunch last week. And he was one of the worst – with stringy, matted hair, a spotted complexion, and lips curled in a permanent sneer.

Becka pressed herself against a wall and watched as he went to his locker. Squinting, she made out the number. As soon as he banged it shut and walked away, she scurried over to it. She glanced around. No one was watching. She squeezed the note into the crack between the locker and its door.

She slowly let out a deep breath. Then she couldn't help smiling. *Forget about being an actress*, she told herself. *You've got a real future as a spy.*

The bleachers were packed and the noise in the gym was deafening. Becka could hardly hear the band, which was playing the school song over and over. Which was just as well, since they weren't very good.

Of course, music wasn't the main thing on her mind. She kept looking around the room. Where was the clown? Probably hiding somewhere, like in the boys' locker room, until it was time to come out.

She was sitting in the front row, right where Heather had told her to sit. Strangely, she wasn't feeling as nervous as she thought she would. Maybe it was because Cat was sitting on one side of her and Josie on the other.

When Josie got up, Becka grabbed her hand. "Where are you going?"

"I just saw Jason, and I want to invite him to the cookout."

"What cookout?"

"Don't you remember? Annie and Ben said we could invite kids over for after the rally."

"I invited Marla and some other kids," Cat told them.

Becka hadn't even thought to invite anyone. Maybe if she ran into those girls from homeroom, and Louise, she'd ask them. Even with

125

everything else on her mind, it was satisfying to know she had people in her life who could be *real* friends.

Suddenly, there was a drumroll, and three people came out on the stage – Dr Potter, a man with a whistle around his neck, and a boy. The boy spoke first. He practically had to scream to be heard over the noise.

"I'm Larry Jacobs, president of the student body." There was a smattering of applause and a few good-natured catcalls. "Welcome to the first pep rally. We're here to show our support for the number one junior high football team in the state of Vermont!"

This statement was greeted with a resounding cheer from the crowd. Larry went on to announce the schedule of games and the opponents. Then he introduced Dr Potter.

Becka barely listened to Dr Potter's speech on teamwork, good sportsmanship, and school spirit. When he finished, he introduced Coach Meadows.

"He looks mean," Becka whispered to Josie.

"He isn't, really," Josie said in a mournful tone. "I'd like to work with him."

Cat leaned across Becka. "You will," she told Josie.

As the coach announced the name of each football player, the team member ran out onto the gym floor to applause. Once they were all out, Larry Jacobs took over again.

"I now present the Green Falls Junior High

cheerleading squad. Here's the captain, Heather Beaumont!"

Heather ran out onto the floor and did a cartwheel. *Land on your rear*, Becka ordered her silently. Of course she didn't. Looking at her objectively, Becka had to admit she looked awfully cute. But . . . "You're prettier than she is," she whispered to Cat.

Cat smiled. Being Cat, she didn't say "thanks." Just, "I know."

Within moments there were eight girls in identical short, blue and white skirts standing in front of the crowd. There was a sense of anticipation in the room. The cheers were about to begin.

Heather stepped forward. "We're going to do something different tonight, and maybe start a new tradition. The honour of leading the first cheer will be given to a new student."

Becka noticed the look of bewilderment on the other cheerleaders' faces. Obviously, they knew nothing about this. *That's a relief*, she thought. At least the entire squad wasn't out to get her.

Heather extended her hands. "And that student is Becka Morgan!"

There was only a little polite applause. Becka wasn't surprised. After all, hardly anyone knew her.

"Come out here, Becka!" Heather called, looking straight at her and smiling. Becka smiled back. She shook her head.

Heather looked puzzled. "Becka, come on!" When Becka still didn't move, Heather started forward, as if she was going to drag Becka onto the floor.

Becka felt Cat poke her in the ribs. "Don't be a wimp!" she whispered. "Get up!"

Becka did. She was amazed to hear how loudly and smoothly she spoke. "Thank you for the honour, Heather. But I don't feel worthy of it. I'm sure the students would much rather hear you lead the first cheer." She sat back down.

Heather stood there uncertainly. Meanwhile, the crowd was getting restless. "Get started!" someone yelled.

Panic crossed Heather's face. Behind her, one of the cheerleaders said, "Come on, Heather, she doesn't want to do it."

"You're holding everything up," another one yelled.

Heather went pale. She moved back to her original position in front of the other cheer-leaders, her head turned towards the far end of the gym. She shook her head violently, mouthing the word *no*. Becka could have sworn her hands were shaking as she raised them in the air, and in a feeble voice, proclaimed, "One, two, three, let's go!"

He seemed to come out of nowhere. Like a streak of lighting, a bike carrying a clown careered across the gym floor. Heather had only enough time to shriek, "No!" before the pie hit her squarely in the face. And there she was, for all the school to see – Heather Beaumont, covered in gooey yellow cream.

For a moment, there was a dead silence. Then the entire crowd began to roar. In Becka's wildest daydreams, she never thought she would see or hear anything so completely satisfying.

Nine

"Just a Diet Coke, please," Cat told the waitress at Luigi's. Then she settled back to wait. She was in a good position; she could see the door, but whoever entered couldn't see her.

So far, so good. To amuse herself while she waited, she conjured up the image of Heather with pie smeared all over her face and dripping from her hair. In that first moment, Cat could have sworn she saw the light from a camera go off. That seemed to jar Heather out of her shocked state, and she ran out of the gym. One of the other cheerleaders took over, and the rally proceeded as if nothing had happened. But when it was over, it was all anyone could talk about.

Cat wished she could have hung around to listen and enjoy her victory. But it was a luxury she couldn't afford. There was more to be done before she could call her scheme a total success.

So much could still go wrong, Cat thought as the waitress set the soda down in front of her. What if Todd didn't stop by his locker after school? What if he went looking for Heather after the rally?

But a lucky star must have been shining on her that day. There he was now, walking in the door. He stood for a moment, looking around the room, then plonked himself down in an empty booth.

Cat picked up her soda and walked over to him. "Mind if I join you?" She didn't wait for a response before sliding into the seat across from him.

"I'm waiting for someone," Todd said.

Cat bowed her head demurely. "Please listen to me, Todd. Just for a minute." She put a little tremble into her voice, so she'd sound like she was fighting back tears.

Todd shifted in his seat uncomfortably. But he didn't say no.

Cat never found it easy to play humble, but that was what the situation called for. "Todd, I *never* called you a pushover. You see, my sister Becka was angry at me about something. So she made that up and told Heather. How . . ." – and she choked up a little – "how could you think I'd ever say something like that about *you*?" She raised her eyes slightly to observe his reaction.

Todd looked a little bewildered. "You never said you had me wrapped around your little finger?"

"Oh, Todd, no! Of course not! It was all Becka's fault."

He drummed his fingers on the table. "Becka . . . Is she the one who was supposed to lead the first cheer at the rally?"

Cat nodded. "She chickened out at the last minute. Lucky for her."

"Yeah. That clown with the pie . . ." He shook his head. "Why would anyone do something like that?"

Boys are so dense, Cat thought. "I have no idea. Poor Heather."

Hearing her name made him look at his watch. He frowned.

"Are you supposed to be meeting her here?" Cat asked.

"Uh, yeah."

"Oh, dear." Cat arranged her features into a sympathetic expression. "Todd, I hate to be the one to tell you this, but I think you've been stood up."

"What are you talking about?"

"Well, on my way here, I walked past Brownies, and I saw Heather . . . with a boy."

Todd's face registered disbelief.

"I wouldn't lie to you, Todd." Cat stood up and rested a hand lightly on his. "Come on, I'll show you."

She kept her fingers crossed as they went down the street. When they reached Brownies, she peered through the window. Her lucky star must have followed her. "There. See?"

Heather's back was to them. As they watched, a geeky greaser went to her table and sat down. Cat couldn't see Heather's expression, but she could imagine it.

"I can't believe this," Todd said. "She stood me up for *him*?"

"There's no accounting for taste," Cat said sadly. She had to get him away from there. Any minute now, Heather would leap up and order the greaser away.

Cat tugged on Todd's arm. "Come on. You don't want to see any more." She dragged him down the street and around the corner. All the while, Todd was shaking his head and saying over and over, "I can't believe this."

"I'm so sorry you had to find out this way," Cat said.

Now Todd was getting angry. "And after what I did for her."

"What did you do?" Cat asked.

He had the grace to look embarrassed. "She said she wouldn't go out with me again unless I told Coach Meadows that the basketball team didn't want any girls. And it wasn't true. I didn't even ask the team. I just told the coach that as a favour to Heather."

Cat made a conscious effort to keep her voice light. "Well, here's your chance to take it back." She pointed to the phone booth on the corner.

Todd scratched his head. "Gee, I feel kind of goofy." He gave Cat a grin that almost melted her heart. Almost, but not quite.

She pushed him towards the phone. "Do it!"

"How many for hot dogs?" Annie asked

the group in the backyard. Four kids raised their hands. "And how many hamburgers?" She counted. "Five. Okay, Ben's firing up the grill now."

Josie stuck a tape into the portable cassette player she'd brought out, and the yard filled with music.

"Where's Cat?" Marla asked.

"She had to take care of something," Josie said. "She'll be here soon."

"Ooh, you've got a horse!" Britt squealed.

Josie gazed over at the far end of the yard where Maybelline was listlessly grazing. "Yeah, if you can call her that." She remembered how thrilled she had been when she first heard that the Morgans had a horse. And how disappointed she was when she discovered that the old mare was the laziest horse in the universe.

Becka came over with two girls. "Josie, this is Patty and this is Lisa. They're in my home-room."

"Hi," Josie said. "There are sodas on the porch if you want some." Patty and Lisa took off in that direction, but Becka lingered.

"Did you invite anyone?" she asked Josie.

"Just Jason and Andie. Who else was I going to invite? Eve?" Josie made a face.

"I don't think Eve knew anything about Heather keeping you off the basketball team," Becka said.

"Yeah, but I'll bet she knew what Heather had planned for you." She punched Becka

134

lightly on the shoulder. "United we stand, divided we fall."

Jason joined them, catching those last words. "Hey, that's pretty cool. You guys really stick together, huh?"

Josie grinned. "Well, today we did."

"All three of you were adopted together, right?" Jason whistled. "That's very interesting. Unusual, too. How would you like to see an article about you in the *Gazette*?"

Becka spoke up. "I'd rather *write* an article."

"You would?" Jason looked at her in surprise. "You want to be on the newspaper staff?"

"Yes," Becka said simply.

"She's a good writer," Josie added.

"Great. Come to the meeting after school on Monday, okay?"

"So that's all it takes," Becka murmured to Josie after he left them.

"What do you mean?"

"All this time I've been waiting for someone to talk to me or to invite me to join them. I was a wimp, just like Cat always said. Well, I'm not going to be one any more."

"Josie!" Annie called from the porch. "Telephone."

Josie went into the house and picked up the phone in the kitchen. "Hello?"

"This is Coach Meadows."

Josie gulped. "Hi. How are you?"

The coach didn't bother with any niceties.

"I've just been informed that the basketball team has changed its mind about you. Practice starts in two weeks."

It took Josie a full minute to recover from the shock. By the time she'd squeaked out a "thank you," he'd already hung up.

Cat rinsed the glass off in the sink and handed it to Becka. "So I just told him, 'Todd, if you ever want to see me again, you call Coach Meadows right this minute.'"

"That's telling him," Becka said in approval.

"Thanks, Cat," Josie said, taking the dried glass from Becka and putting it in the cupboard.

"I really came through for you guys today," Cat went on. "But you better not expect that all the time. You can't depend on me to take care of you."

"Who asked you to do that?" Josie asked indignantly.

"All I'm saying is that you have to stand up for yourselves from now on."

Annie and Ben came into the kitchen. "You girls have done a great job cleaning up," Annie said.

"Listen, kids," Ben said, "I want to pick up the paint for the bedroom tomorrow. It's the last day of the sale. But I need to know what colour the occupant is going to want. So you better make a decision tonight."

"Why don't you go up to your room and talk it over," Annie suggested. "Come up with the reasons why you each think you should have the private room. Then, if you still can't agree on who has the best reasons, come back and talk to us."

The girls went up to their room. They each sat down on their own bed, and Cat spoke first. "I think I should get the room."

"Why?" Josie asked.

"First of all, because I have more friends than either of you, so I'll have more company. And sleepovers. Second, after what I did for you guys today, you owe me a favour."

Josie sneered. "You didn't do all that just for us. You wanted revenge on Heather yourself. And you wanted to get Todd back."

Becka offered her opinion. "Besides, a private bedroom is a pretty big reward for two little favours."

"Little!" Cat glared at her. "If it wasn't for me, Josie wouldn't be on that basketball team. And you'd be the laughing stock of Green Falls Junior High. You'd be in the bathroom right now still washing pie out of your hair. What a couple of ingrates."

"Look, we said thanks," Josie said.

"Big deal," Cat snorted. "If you're really thankful, you'll let me have the new bedroom." She turned to Josie. "What's your reason for wanting the bedroom?"

Josie fell back on her bed. "My main reason

is so that I don't have to listen to you and Becka squabbling."

"Well, if I get the room, that will solve your problem," Cat noted.

"True," Josie admitted.

"Then it's settled," Cat said, looking pleased. "I get the room."

"Not so fast," Becka said. "*I* want the room."

"*You!*" Cat glared at her in the way that usually made Becka cower. Not this time, though.

"Yes. And I've got the best reason. I study more than either of you and I need the quiet and the privacy."

"A private room just to study?" Cat exclaimed. "What a waste!"

Becka smiled. "I'll bet Annie and Ben won't think so."

Cat was gaping at her as if she were a total stranger. Becka explained, "I'm just doing what you told me to do. I'm standing up for myself."

"She's got a point," Josie said to Cat. "And I think she's got the best reason."

"Whose side are you on?" Cat demanded.

"I thought we were all on the same side," Becka said. "You said so yourself."

"That was under special conditions," Cat proclaimed.

There was a rap on the door. Annie stuck her head in. "I don't see any blood. Have you guys come to a decision?"

While she was still feeling courageous, Becka

spoke quickly. "I think I should have the room, because I read and study a lot and I need the quiet."

"Do you agree?" Annie asked, looking at Cat and Josie.

Josie gave a noncommittal shrug. Cat just grimaced.

"Then that's settled," Annie said. "What colour do you want the room, Becka?"

"Pale pink," Becka said promptly.

"Okay. Now why don't you guys come on down and we'll make some popcorn?"

Josie left with Annie. Cat sat there for a moment and stared at Becka. Becka stared right back and tried to read her expression. Was it possibly respect?

Maybe. If it was, it probably wouldn't last. She had to be realistic. Nothing changed overnight. Josie would go on teasing her, Cat would go on insulting her. But she'd taken a step. A giant one.

Cat rose. "Who do you think you are?" She muttered, walking out the door.

"I'm Becka Morgan," Becka said to the empty room. And for the first time in a long time, she felt like that wasn't such a bad person to be.

Here's a sneak peek at what's ahead in the exciting fourth book of THREE OF A KIND: *Two's Company, Four's a Crowd.*

"Listen," Cat said suddenly. "Don't tell anyone about the letter from my secret admirer, okay?"

"Not even Josie?" Becka asked.

"Especially not Josie. She'll just tease me and make jokes about it."

"You're right," Becka agreed. "Josie wouldn't understand. I don't think she knows anything about romance."

"But she could," Cat mused. "You know, all she and Red need is a little push."

"Are *you* thinking about giving them the push?"

Cat grinned. "Why not? If Josie fell in love, she'd be a lot more feminine. And a lot easier to live with."

They heard Ben's call to dinner from downstairs.

"Now remember what I said," Cat cautioned as they ran down the stairs. "Not a word about you-know-what."

"Not a word," Becka promised. Having Cat's

confidence gave her a warm glow. It wasn't too long ago that they couldn't bear to be in the same room. Becka and Cat joined Annie, Ben, and Josie at the table. Becka cast an appreciative eye on the main course.

"Mmm, chicken pie."

"How was your day, girls?" Ben asked.

"We had a great basketball practice," Josie reported. "Oh, Cat, Todd said to tell you he'd call tonight."

"Okay," Cat said.

"Cat, don't you like your chicken pie?" Annie asked anxiously.

"What? Oh, sure, it's great. I guess I'm just not very hungry."

"Uh-oh," Ben said. "Isn't loss of appetite a sign of being in love?"

"Not for me," Annie said cheerfully. "Every time I fell in love, I ate like a pig. When I first met Ben, I gained five pounds."

"Maybe Becka's in love, then," Josie remarked.

Becka looked at her plate and flushed when she realised she'd already devoured her pie. Annie and Ben were looking at her with interest.

"Well, there is a boy I kind of like," she confessed.

"Who is he?" Ben asked.

"Now, Ben, don't pry," Annie chided him. "When Becka wants to tell us about him, she will."

"It'll be interesting to see how Josie reacts to being in love," Ben said in a teasing voice.

"I'll be sick to my stomach," Josie replied promptly.

"Josie!" Cat exclaimed. "Not at the table, *please*!"

"Don't worry. It's not going to happen any time soon. If ever."

Cat turned her head and gave Becka a significant wink.

"What's going on at school?" Annie asked.

"There's going to be a dance," Cat said.

Annie clapped her hands. "Your first dance! Oh, we have to go shopping."

"For what?" Ben asked.

"Ben! We've got three daughters going to their first dance! Three daughters means three new outfits."

"Not three," Josie said. "I'm not going."

"How do you know?" Cat said. "Maybe Red will ask you."

Josie made a face.

"Are you going, Becka?" Annie asked.

"If somebody asks me."

"You mean, you have to have a date?" Ben asked.

"You don't have to," Cat told him. "But everybody does."

Annie shook her head. "Kids grow up so fast nowadays."

After dinner, the girls cleared the table. Once they were alone in the kitchen, Josie turned to Becka. "Who's this boy you kind of like?"

Cat answered for her. "Keith Doyle."

"Keith Doyle! Gross!"

"What's gross about him?" Becka asked indignantly.

"I heard some of the guys talking about him. They said he plays around, he flirts with everyone. He gets girls to fall madly in love with him."

"Oh, *please*," Cat snorted. "All boys do that." Her eyes grew misty. "Until they get older. Then, one day, they find their one-and-only, now-and-forever love."

Josie brushed that aside. "I heard worse about Keith Doyle. There's a rumour that he cheats."

"I don't believe that," Becka said stoutly. "If he cheated, he wouldn't be making Ds in French."

"What's the big deal, anyway?" Cat challenged Josie. "Okay, maybe he cheats a little. So what? He's cute, and he's popular, and Becka likes him. So mind your own business!"

"I'm just warning her," Josie countered. "You gotta watch out for guys like that. If you ask me, he sounds kind of sleazy."

"Nobody asked you," Cat shot back.

"C'mon, you guys, stop it," Becka pleaded. "Look, he hasn't even asked me out."

"*Yet*," Cat added.

Josie threw up her hands and went back out to the dining room. Becka stared after her thoughtfully. "You know, Cat, I think you're right about Josie."

"Right about what?"

"She *does* need to fall in love."